AGINCOURT

Jenkin Lloyd, France 1415

by Michael Cox

D1589930

To Ted Cox
(3rd April 1923 – 10th November 2002)

Scholastic Children's Books
Commonwealth House, 1–19 New Oxford Street,
London, WC1A 1NU, UK
A division of Scholastic Ltd
London ~ New York ~ Toronto ~ Sydney ~ Auckland
Mexico City ~ New Delhi ~ Hong Kong

Published in the UK by Scholastic Ltd, 2003

Copyright © Michael Cox, 2003

All rights reserved

ISBN 0 439 98266 9

Printed and bound in Denmark by
Nørhaven Paperback, Viborg

Cover image supplied by Andy Lubienski
Background image supplied by Mary Evans Picture Library

2 4 6 8 10 9 7 5 3

December 1415

My name is Jenkin Lloyd and I live in the village of Tregarth in the Welsh lordship of Nether Gwent. I am fourteen years old and this is my story.

Sometimes, when my companions and I are gathered round the fire on these freezing winter nights, I think back on our great adventure and I can still hardly believe it all took place. But then I notice the partly healed scars on my right arm where the Frenchman's war-hammer tore my flesh, and I look to my friends and see the empty place where one of us no longer sits. Each night, as I close my eyes to sleep, I once more see the sky darken as our arrows blot out the pale October sun and I hear the screams of the dying men and horses again. And then I know for certain that I was there.

3

1401 – August 1415

I was born in Tregarth some fourteen years ago and I have lived there almost all of my life with my parents and my sister, Gwynn. Ever since I reached an age when I could be trusted to toddle to our henhouse and collect the eggs without dropping them, or to lead our plough horse up to the pasture by the millstream without its enormous hooves crushing my little feet, I've worked on our tiny plot of land and our lord Cradok's great estate from dawn till dusk, day in, day out. My jobs are many and never-ending and, as with all things in our constant struggle for survival, they are governed by the seasons. In the spring I till the earth and scare the birds from the newly planted corn. In summer I weed the crops and reap the harvest. In autumn-time I plough the land and collect the fire-wood that will help us endure our long, hard Welsh winters. Then, at Christmastide, when the snow lies thick on the ground and the bitter gales howl around our little cottage, I break the thick ice that covers our well and slaughter the pig which has grown fat on the acorns and beech nuts that litter our local forests. These are just a few of my tasks, and almost of all of them I learned from my father, William Lloyd.

Being the most learned man in the district, my father not only worked alongside the rest of us on the land but was also employed by our lord, Cradok, in the counting of his stock and the keeping of his records. It was from him that I learned my reading and writing and my understanding of the English tongue.

Like all of the men in our village and, for that matter, all of south-east Wales, my father had also been an archer, and had served under Lord Cradok in the wars against the English. Ever since I was small I can remember seeing him and the other men of the village standing on the green each Sunday, practising their skills, my father holding the great bow that had been his father's before him and his grandfather's before that. Then, when I was just six years old, my father gave me my own bow and I joined him at archery practice. Sometimes we would go into the woods and take shots at birds or wild boar. But, like all the other men and boys from our district, most of our training was done at the butts that stood near our village church. These are the targets that are now in every town and village in England and Wales and that all boys and men must regularly practise at each Sunday, on the orders of our King. We were joined by many more archers from the surrounding farms and hamlets and by my childhood playmates: the twins, Owen and Morgan Bowen, my cousin and best friend, Harry Price, and by plucky Evan Lewis, who would always be with his uncle, Wynn Vaughn.

Under the eagle eyes of my father, Wynn and the other men, my little friends and I were taught to become archers. My father would stand over me, smiling at my childish excitement and beginner's clumsiness as I notched my arrow to the greased string of my bow. Then, as I struggled to stretch the string back to my ear, he would give me warm words of encouragement and advice. Finally, having sighted my arrow on the target, I would loose my shaft. Sometimes it would fly wide of the mark but, as I grew and practised, I quickly gained in confidence and skill. Soon I was competing with my friends to see who could hit the bull's eye the most, or who could loose off most arrows in a given time. And occasionally, as a change from butt shooting, I would clout shoot. To do this I would put a piece of cloth on the ground, then, from some distance, I would fire my arrows high into the air, attempting to land them on the cloth. Not easy, but excellent training for the battlefield … as my story will show.

In the evening, after archery practice or working in the fields, my father would sit by the fire with me and tell me enthralling tales of the battles that he and his fellow Welsh archers had fought against the English in the years before I was born. One tale I never tired of hearing was about a fight that had taken place quite near Tregarth, during which a mounted English knight had charged at my father as he struggled to fit an arrow to his bow. Just when it looked as if the knight would skewer him on his lance, Wynn Vaughn had put an arrow into the knight's thigh. Such was the power of the shot that it not only penetrated the man's leg armour and his leg, but passed through his thigh and went into the flank of his horse. And then, as the soldier turned to flee, my father loosed his own arrow, striking the knight in his other thigh. Again, the arrow passed through both flesh and armour, pinning that leg to the knight's horse too!

After listening to tales like this, firing my bow and becoming a skilled archer became the thing I wanted more than anything in the world. At every spare moment, I could be found loosing off my arrows at a little wooden target my father had set up in the meadow behind our cottage. As well as constantly improving my shooting skills, I also learned about the making of our bows. My father told me how the best of them are made from the wood of the yew tree, which is the strongest and springiest of all wood, and how, as the whole of Wales is not covered in an everlasting supply of yew trees, our bowyers make four bows from elm, wych-hazel or ash wood for each one they make of yew. And among the many other things he showed me was how our arrows are put together. Each one is made from a smooth shaft of ash wood, tipped at one end with a razor-sharp steel "bodkin" spike and at the other with feathers from a duck, goose or peacock, to ensure that it flies straight and true.

Over the coming months and years I do not know how many countless thousands of times I pulled back my bowstring, but soon the muscles of my pulling arm and left shoulder grew big and strong, out of all proportion to those of my other arm, just as they did on all experienced archers. Of course, I couldn't be practising all of the time, as my duties on our farm were increasing each year, but I quickly began to gain a reputation as a first-class bowman, soon being able to loose off some twelve arrows in just one minute, as all of our best archers could.

And then, when I was eleven years old, tragedy struck and my father was thrown from his horse one bitter winter's night. After lying by the roadside for many hours he was found, half frozen, and brought to our cottage. Five hours later he died from his injuries and of the cold. As we stood by his bedside some minutes before he passed away, he whispered to me to fetch his bow. Then, as I leaned close to him, he told me that it was now mine and that I must make myself worthy of it and all those who had owned it before me.

On a warm July evening in this year of 1415, I was sitting outside my mother's cottage with Evan, the Bowens and Harry. That day, we'd all been hard at work in the fields near our village and now we were taking our ease, discussing the wart that had recently sprouted on Owen's chin, and how it would be so very useful to tell him apart from his twin. But then we saw Evan's uncle, Wynn Vaughn, striding towards us with a strange and agitated look upon his face. Our carefree mood soon vanished as he gave us the news that would change our lives for ever.

"Boys," said Wynn, "I have something to tell you that may fill your hearts with fear – or possibly with gladness and excitement. But, whichever way you receive it, I have to tell you that all of you will shortly be setting out on an adventure that you could never have imagined in your wildest dreams. An adventure that may bring you glory and riches. Or at worst, pain and death."

"So!" joked Morgan Bowen. "Are we to raid some distant valley and steal sheep?"

"No," said Wynn. "You are to go to war."

At these words the smiles fell from our faces and we looked at one another as though we believed Wynn might be playing some sort of trick on us.

"To war!" said Owen Bowen, his eyes as big as plates. "What! With the English?"

"No!" said Wynn. "Our quarrels with the English are at an end. We are to fight the French. And we are to fight them on their own soil. Henry, King of England and Prince of Wales, has demanded they give him what he believes is his. In other words, the right to rule all France. And they have refused. So the King is to claim his birthright by force. He is now mustering a great army for that purpose. Our lord Cradok has pledged six archers to join that army. We are those six archers.

"In five days we will leave our village and make our way to the English county of Hampshire where we will join the King's army and the Welsh archers led by Davy Gam. Then we are to sail for France."

I cannot begin to tell you how much of a shock this news was to me. I was immediately gripped by feelings of sweaty terror and dark foreboding, but mixed with my stomach-churning fear was a sense of excitement at the great undertaking that lay before me. In the fourteen years that I had lived, the only things I had known were ploughing, sowing, reaping, caring for our animals and practising my archery. And I had never travelled further than our neighbouring villages, all no more than some six miles distant. Now, not only was I to journey hundreds of miles from my home and family, but I was to cross the sea to a foreign land. And then I would take part in a war there – a war in which I might earn honours and riches or be horribly wounded and possibly even lose my life!

In the recent past our fathers and grandfathers had fought many battles with both the English and their fellow Welshmen. But, since King Henry V had come to the throne, much of Wales had been at peace with England. Indeed, many Welshmen had high regard for the daring young English king who had once fought against them so courageously. And now I was to help this brave king in an enterprise so huge and so daunting that just to think of it made me feel as small and pathetic as the flies which crawled across our cottage ceiling.

So maybe you can understand why I did not sleep the night we got our news. Nor the next! And why I tossed and turned for hours, not only wondering what sort of places the countries of England and France might be, but also trying to picture what a real Frenchman might actually look like.

Five days later, as a thrush sang in the apple tree outside our cottage and our hens clucked and scraped at the kitchen floor, I pulled on my leather boots, bowman's gloves and the short-sleeved tunic they call a jack. I then put on my steel bowman's cap, or bascinet, as it is usually known, and picked up the pack containing my spare clothes, water bottle, food and the cloak I would use when it rained and for sleeping. Finally, I gathered up my father's bow and my various other weapons, then stepped out of our front door. After hugging my mother and sister and saying my goodbyes to them and our old dog, Gryff, I joined Wynn Vaughn and my pals on our village green. Our friends and neighbours had all gathered to wish us well. With their cheery farewells ringing in our ears, the six of us crossed the old wooden bridge by the church, took the road through the woods, and began our journey.

As my companions and I walked away from our village on that sunny August morning, I grasped my bow, feeling the smooth coolness of its yew wood and its wonderful springy strength. Then, remembering the words my father had uttered with his dying breath, I silently vowed to myself that, whatever dangers and terrors came my way during the coming weeks and months, I would endeavour to prove myself worthy of this mighty weapon.

It took us ten days to walk to the part of the English coast where King Henry had chosen to gather his great invasion fleet. It was at a place called Spithead, quite near the town of Southampton. But, because the fleet and army were so huge, the loading of the ships was to take place along a stretch of coastline many miles long.

During our march the weather stayed warm and dry, so we slept comfortably in the barns and haystacks we found along the way and were not troubled by our lack of tents or other shelter. Sometimes, as we trudged through a village, someone would ask us where we were bound and, after Wynn had told them in his very best English, they would bring us out some bread and cheese, or offer us their good wishes for success in our adventure. But often this didn't happen at all. Villagers would ignore us completely, or set their dogs on us.

As the days passed we began to see more and more groups of men and boys just like ourselves, all trudging along the hot and dusty lanes that led to the English coast. And just like us, they were dressed in jacks and gloves made from boiled leather and they carried the traditional weapons of the archer. From the belts above their cloth breeches hung their small shields, along with the swords and war-hammers that they would use in close-quarters fighting. On their backs they carried their great, six-foot-long bows, while at their waists, or in their quivers, were their arrows. As I nodded my greetings to my fellow bowmen, it suddenly came to me that in towns and hamlets all over the Kingdom there must be many

14

hundreds of us. Boys and men who, just like me, had spent long hours practising their archery skills at their own village butts in preparation for an event such as this.

Each night, as we lay under hedgerows or in sweet-smelling haylofts and Owen Bowen snored and grunted like some hog, I would lie awake, remembering the things my mother had told me about the king who would soon lead us into battle. How she had told me that from the age of thirteen he had fought so bravely in campaigns in Scotland, Wales and Ireland; how he could outrun a full-grown deer, then wrestle it to the ground; and how he was not only a talented musician, but also a speaker of many languages. I also remembered how she had said he was an inquisitive and restless man whose love of reading and quest for knowledge was such that he would always take away the book collections of any towns or great houses he captured so that he might add to his store of wisdom. Then I would long for the day when I would finally catch sight of this glorious leader of men.

As our march took us further south we entered immense forests filled with giant oak and beech trees. These forests were alive with wild creatures and, as we made our way down wooded chases, splashed through streams, and tramped along twisting pathways, wild boar ran grunting and squealing into the undergrowth. In the trees above us, squirrels leaped from branch to branch, jays screamed and woodpeckers hammered, intent on their noisy search for insects.

It was in these vast stretches of woodland, or the New Forest, as the English called it, that we began to come across clearings filled with signs of human activity: carpets of sawdust, piles of curly wood-shavings and smouldering heaps of twigs and branches, all standing alongside hundreds and hundreds of tree stumps, still bright with the marks of the foresters' axes.

"The King's shipbuilders have been busy," said Wynn, as we perched on a circle of these stumps and ate our bread. "His desire for boats to take his army across the English Channel is very great." Then he paused and smiled, adding, "So great indeed that not only have his shipwrights been busy turning the stout oaks of these forests into new vessels, but I've heard that he's also taken ships from recently arrived Dutch and Italian seafarers.

They say that he now has 1,500 boats lying at anchor, all of them intended for France."

"Well, that is a relief!" roared Owen Bowen, playfully elbowing little Harry Price in the ribs so hard that he fell from his tree-stump perch. "For I remember Harry here telling me that we would all be expected to *swim* to France!"

As we laughed at his plight, Harry leaped up from the turf. And, like the little scrapper he was, my best friend hurled himself at the much larger boy and soon the two of them were wrestling ferociously, rolling around and around the forest floor. As Wynn, Evan and Morgan all cheered and clapped their antics, my own mind began to wander and I thought about the sea we were soon to cross.

I wondered just how it might look and how deep and wide it might be. I decided that when I did finally set eyes upon this ocean I would remember every detail of it so that on my return to Tregarth I could tell my mother and my sister of this wondrous thing I had seen.

We now had only some eighteen miles to go before we reached our destination. Soon it seemed that we couldn't come to a crossroads or village without being joined by more and more groups of fighting-men, all making their way towards Spithead and the King's great war-fleet. The roads became filled with long columns of archers, stretching as far as the eye could see. Many of them, like us, were on foot, but others were mounted on spirited little horses and ponies which also carried their packs, weapons and sheaves of arrows. As these mounted archers trotted by, I looked at them with envy, wishing I had a horse like theirs. I tried to imagine what it would be like to charge into battle on such a mount, twisting this way and that as I loosed off one arrow after another at my helpless foes.

It was about this time that we began to encounter proud knights riding their magnificent warhorses through the leafy lanes of Hampshire. Most of them had not yet put on the armour they would wear in battle, content to have it carried on their baggage wagons and pack horses. But some, no doubt eager for the fight, or anxious to make a grand impression, were already encased from head to toe in beautifully burnished steel plate that gleamed and glinted in the bright August sunshine. I gazed at their perfectly polished helmets, glittering breast and back plates, jointed leg-guards, elbow and shoulder protectors and their steel shoes. These were so sharp-toed that I truly believed they might have been able to kill a man with just one kick. And then, as my eyes fell upon the fearsome lances, poleaxes and mallets which they grasped in their iron-studded, steel-gauntleted hands, I realized that our enemies would have similar weapons. I wondered what it might be like to be run though or maimed by such arms, and my blood ran cold.

With haughty warning cries of "Make way! Make way!" these knights would come galloping up behind us, carelessly forcing their way through our ranks, causing us to leap aside as their huge mounts kicked up choking clouds of dust and grit. Moments later, their grooms and pages and strings of replacement warhorses would follow in their wake, once more showering us with dirt from their wildly flailing hooves.

It wasn't only fighting-men that swarmed along the highways and byways of southern England during those days before our embarkation. Alongside all this soldiery, I began to see teams of heavy horses pulling wagons piled high with provisions: red-raw sides of beef, enormous yellow cheeses, loaves of crusty bread, barrels of ale, clothes, armour, timber, medicines … everything the King's army would need to survive the campaign.

Huge herds of livestock also wandered along the lanes: cows, pigs, geese and noisy flocks of sheep and lambs, many of which were breeds I'd never seen before. These various beasts were urged on by their grumbling drovers and the quick-tempered dogs that ran between their feet, constantly growling and snapping at their heels.

"There goes next week's dinner, lads!" said Wynn Vaughn as a couple of farmboys chased past us in hot pursuit of a bullock. It had taken fright when a group of Welshmen some distance behind us had loudly and unexpectedly burst into song.

On the final morning of our journey, just after we'd passed a sign telling us that the town of Southampton was some ten miles distant, a strong breeze blew up. I caught a whiff of a strange smell, the likes of which had never entered my nostrils before. It was a sharp, tangy smell that reminded me a little of the salted sides of bacon which my ma hung in our cellar in readiness for the hunger of the winter months. A few minutes later we passed through a small wood and crested a rise. Then, emerging from the cool shade of the trees into the bright early light, I realized where that salty tang had come from. For the first time in my life, I looked upon that immense body of water they call the sea. I thought my eyes might pop from their sockets, so great was my astonishment. The vast ocean lay spread below us like newly polished armour, rippling and twinkling in the summer sunshine as if covered with countless tiny jewels. Dotted all about it, and looking for all the world like the red, gold and brown leaves that bob and swirl on Tregarth's streams and ponds every autumn-time, were hundreds and hundreds of wooden boats. In every bay and creek there were ships and barges of every imaginable sort, their sails billowing and their pennants fluttering – the King's war-fleet of which Wynn had spoken earlier.

It was mid-morning when we finally made our way along the dusty road that led to the quaysides. Here we were to board a wooden barge that would ferry us to France. As we neared the shoreline our little group was soon swallowed up by a vast multitude of soldiers, horses, baggage-boys and anxious-looking royal officials, who yelled and rushed this way and that, trying to bring some sort of order to the chaos around us. In all my life I had never seen so many people gathered in one place. Everywhere I looked there was movement and noise. Horses whinnied and stamped, men shouted and laughed, dogs barked and sergeants roared orders at marching men. And there, rocking gently at their moorings by the jetties, in all shapes and sizes, were dozens of brightly painted boats and barges. I watched in amazement as barefoot sailors ran across their decks, hauled on ropes and unfurled canvas sails. They dashed up and down their rigging as nimbly and effortlessly as I had seen those squirrels dash up and down the oaks in the forest. Soon, I thought proudly, I would be aboard one of these great vessels, on my way to a foreign land where I would earn honour and glory in the name of my King, my God, and my father.

We shortly came to a grassy hillock not far from the quayside and it was here that Wynn told us to take our rest until it was time for us to join our fellow Welsh archers and board our barge. So, unslinging our bows and packs, we sat down and set about attending to our weapons and sorting our equipment. But we couldn't help occasionally pausing to wonder at the hubbub of activity that was taking place before us.

"You'd think we were going to a banquet," said Morgan, as we watched bakers and butchers staggering up the ships' gangplanks with baskets of loaves and pig carcasses, millers lugging swollen sacks of flour and draymen rolling the huge barrels of ale which clattered so thunderously across the decking.

"No, not a banquet ... a war!" said Wynn, pointing to the lines of men who carried all manner of weapons, armour and barrels of gunpowder onto the next ship. "Don't be fooled by the sight of all that food and ale, boys. There are 8,000 archers and 1,000 knights in this army who will soon make short work of it, including our very own Welsh eating-machines here, Owen and Morgan Bowen!"

"And let's hope," said Owen, affectionately patting his enormous stomach, "that we'll also make short work of every single Frenchman we meet along the way!"

"As surely as there are Welshmen in Wales, you will!" laughed Wynn. Then he pointed to a spot further along the shoreline where dozens of sweating labourers were attempting to load monstrous wooden catapults onto another, much larger boat. "See, boys, those are the siege machines the King will use to batter any French town that dares to halt our progress!" Wynn cried. "And beyond them are the great cannon: the King's Daughter, the Messenger and London, all newly forged at Bristol and the Tower. They will blast the Frenchies to kingdom come! It's said they're so fearsome they even terrify the gunners who operate them!"

When I saw the three gigantic cannon being dragged towards the quayside by teams of straining horses I couldn't believe that it was possible to make such guns. These terrible weapons looked as though they had been forged by a race of giants in some hellish workshop deep beneath the earth's surface. The barrel of each one must have been at least twelve feet long and their muzzles looked wide enough to hold a man ... if not one of the huge horses that pulled them!

"What monsters!" gasped Evan. "With such fearsome weapons surely the King has no need of archers and men-at-arms."

"But won't the French have such weapons too?" I said. "I hate to think what a blast of stone shot from guns like those could do to a man!"

"Well, Jenkin," said Harry, "if such a thing did happen, all you could do was pray that your end might be swift. The pain that would come with such wounds would surely be unbearable."

"Harry," I said, giving him a reassuring pat on his shoulder, "you must not fear these things. I will be watching over you to see that no such harm befalls you, dear cousin."

"And me you, Jenkin," said Harry, with an affectionate grin.

It seemed that the great procession of stores and weaponry would never end. But finally it did. And then it was time for us to board our own barge. Gathering our kit and weapons, we approached the wooden jetty.

"Won't be long now, boys!" laughed Wynn, as we joined the waiting archers. "I hope you've packed your sea legs!"

As Wynn spoke I caught sight of a pale shape dashing through the ranks of fighting-men who shuffled and fidgeted on the quayside. At first I took it to be one of the animals being loaded onto the ships to provide us with fresh meat during our campaign, possibly a pig, or ram? But an instant later I realized that it was not an escaped hog at all ... but a small and wild-looking man! He suddenly halted and was joined by four or five similar-looking warriors. All of them had wild, staring eyes and great tangled beards. Their exposed flesh was covered in all manner of strange patterns and drawings. Every one of these ferocious-looking folk was armed. In one hand they clutched bundles of short, sharpened sticks, which looked like some sort of throwing spear, and in the other they held enormous knives. They stared wildly about them, almost as if daring someone to challenge them. Then they began to talk among themselves in a language that somehow seemed familiar to me, but also strange and foreign.

"Who are they?" I whispered, staring in disbelief and amazement.

"I'm not sure," said Wynn, "but they certainly are a fearsome-looking mob!"

A grizzled old Welsh archer standing quite close to us spoke up. "Those are Irishmen. Come to help the King in his conquest of France. Wherever there is war there are Irishmen. They are said to love battle and death like other men love money and property. Some say they are totally without fear and rush into battle completely naked, believing that Morrigan, their ancient battle goddess, will protect them from all danger."

"Well," I said, as we watched the wild men swarm aboard their barge, "I'm glad they're fighting on our side!"

"And see," said the ancient archer, pointing beyond the Irishmen, "there are yet more foreigners! Flemish spearmen come to help King Henry in the hope that they'll return to their homes in the Low Countries weighed down with more plunder than they can carry!"

"They can have their plunder!" muttered Morgan Bowen. "As long as they leave the hostage-taking to us! My brother and I are planning to capture a rich French merchant, then sell him back to his family for his weight in gold."

"Or better still," joked Owen, "*our* weight in gold!"

"Well, *I* would like some plunder!" cried Evan, getting more excited by the moment. "I hear a man can become rich overnight, simply from all the loot there is to be had from those rich French manor houses and farms!"

"I may not earn huge ransoms or even manage to bring home a great mountain of booty," said Harry, "but if I can act courageously on the battlefield and earn honour and glory for myself and my country, that will be reward enough for me."

"Bravely spoken, cousin!" I cried. "And that goes for me too. I cannot wait to show those Frenchies what sort of stuff we Welsh lads are made of!" But as I said this, deep in my heart I felt a shiver of fear and wondered if, one day soon, our brave words might not come back to haunt us.

"Well, boys," said Harry, "even if our grand plans come to nothing, at least we all have the six pence a day the King is paying us to be in this army of his."

27

The line of Welsh archers who stood in front of us began to shuffle up the gangplank. As we followed them, I spied a small, dark-haired archer with a black patch over one eye. He was standing on the quayside some yards away from us talking to a tall and muscular nobleman with long white hair and a white beard.

"See, lad!" said the old archer, grabbing my arm. "There is our leader and fellow Welshman, one-eyed Davy Gam. He lost that eye fighting against the English. And the tall nobleman he is talking to is Sir Thomas Erpingham, Commander of all the King's archers. Not so long ago those two were sworn enemies, but now they are united against the French. We could not wish for two better or more experienced leaders. Davy Gam fought alongside our own Welsh warrior, Owen Glyn Dwr, and Sir Thomas battled against Owen and Davy in Wales."

"So he'll know that Welsh archers are the best in all the land!" said Morgan Bowen.

"I'm sure of it!" chuckled the old man. "And if he doesn't, he soon will!"

Ten minutes later, our barge left the shore and, as the waves gently slapped at its creaking timbers and seabirds wheeled and called above us, it made its way out into the waters they call the Solent. Then we turned and moved east, following the line of the shore where we could see dozens more boats also leaving their moorings. After hugging the coast for some miles we reached the port of Spithead and I saw the vast fleet that was gathering around the King's flagship. It put me in mind of hundreds of ducklings flocking around their great and gaudy mother duck. The flagship was called *La Trinité Royale* and I can honestly say that it was one of the most beautiful things I have ever set eyes upon in my whole life. From its four enormous wooden masts there billowed huge sails, all of them brilliantly painted with blue, scarlet and gold falcons, lions and eagles, while hundreds of flags and pennants fluttered from almost every part of the woodwork that covered its various decks. Knowing that King Henry himself would be aboard this vessel, I strained my eyes, anxious to catch a glimpse of this English warrior-hero who was to lead us to victory over our French enemies. But I was disappointed; the ship was too far away for me to see faces and figures properly. Even if I had been able to, it would have been useless, as I had no idea at all what the King might look like.

It was now time for our departure. As the priests who lined the quayside chanted solemnly, drums began to beat, then trumpets sounded, first on one vessel and then the next, until the bright, hot air of the afternoon was ringing with their brassy flourishes. Then, almost unnoticeably at first, the ships of our fleet began to move away from the land. Minutes later, I saw the crowd on the shoreline appear to shrink and I realized that our own vessel was also moving out to sea and, even though every single one of them was a stranger to me, I began waving furiously at the cheering throng. And then, just when I was thinking that my heart could swell no further with the joy and pride of this moment, I heard a shout and saw that everyone was staring skywards. Flying over us, their great wings beating effortlessly and their slender necks stretched before them, was a flock of magnificent white swans.

"It is an omen!" I heard someone cry. "A sign of good fortune! The swan is an emblem of the royal house of Lancaster. God is on the side of our King!"

"Let us hope so!" said Owen Bowen.

"I am sure of it," said Wynn. "The King himself has said that this campaign is God's will."

As the quayside receded even further, he paused, then added. "So … this is it, boys. Our great adventure is finally about to begin."

"Yes," said Harry. "Let us pray we survive whatever

30

perils await us. So that we may tell our families of our great deeds and…"

Harry didn't finish. Suddenly there was a commotion on the seaward side of our barge and men began rushing towards the sides of the boat and pointing at the part of the fleet where the ships were at their closest.

"What is it? What is it?" I cried, overcome by blind panic, fearing that our enemy had somehow come amongst us.

"Look!" cried Owen, pointing to one of the vessels that lay quite close to us. "They are on fire!"

I looked to the boat and saw clouds of smoke billowing from its deck.

"It's the brazier!" I heard one of the sailors shout. "The swell has made the ship lurch, causing it to topple. See! The hot coals have tumbled from it and now the deck is well and truly alight. And the blaze is spreading."

He was right. Fanned by the wind that was to carry us to France, the flames licked greedily at the ship's tar-covered timbers. As they did, I watched the sailors and soldiers on board the burning vessel rush this way and that, not seeming to know what to do. Then, as they looked on helplessly, the blaze engulfed their mainsail with a huge roar. In seconds, the whole vessel was overwhelmed by fire. All at once there was a deafening explosion and a flash and the entire vessel instantly disappeared in a cloud of smoke and flames. The flames had reached the ship's gunpowder stores. Bits of burning timber, hot metal and, I fear to say, the body parts of those very men who had been rushing around in panic just seconds before, flew in all directions. As if this wasn't a terrible enough disaster to begin our great enterprise, some of the burning timbers fell onto two of the ships that were sailing closest to the stricken vessel. Instantly, little fires broke out all over these boats too. Although the men aboard them made haste to put out the blazes, these ships were also soon alight from stem to stern. Realizing that all was lost, sailors and soldiers threw themselves into the sea, some with their clothes and hair already on fire. My heart went out to those poor men as I imagined the agonies they must be going through. And it was at this moment that we heard a terrible inhuman screaming sound and smelled burning flesh.

"Look!" cried Owen. "The horses! The horses! The wretched things are trapped by the fire!"

"Oh no!" gasped Harry, who loved all creatures. "Those poor animals. They don't stand a chance."

The horses aboard the burning vessels were kicking and rearing in their stalls, as sparks and pieces of burning sailcloth showered down on them, scorching their flesh and causing their manes and tails to catch alight. Despite my fear I was suddenly overcome by an urge to hurl myself into the waves and go to their rescue. But it would have been impossible to aid the beasts, even if I had managed to reach the boats. We could only stand by and watch helplessly as the blazing vessels began to disintegrate, causing both burning animals and men to plunge wildly into the sea, where they thrashed about before sinking beneath the waves.

"Oh, this is terrible!" gasped Evan. "Those men and horses must be in agony!"

"What a disaster!" groaned Morgan Bowen, as we watched the ships burn to the waterline. "This is not good! I fear it's an omen sent to tell us our expedition is doomed."

"You must not be so faint-hearted!" said Wynn. "We are going to war. Such things happen. I am sure many more terrors and mishaps will befall the King's army before this adventure is finally over. Look to your courage and your pride. You must all face each horror like the brave Welsh boys you are. I am sure our noble

King is not prepared to see this early misfortune as some sort of terrible warning omen either. After all, these were only three boats out of a great fleet."

It would seem that the crowds on the quayside thought as Wynn did. As the last of the glowing ships' timbers spluttered and hissed angrily, then sank beneath the waves, and small boats rowed out to pick up the surviving men and animals, the onlookers once more began their yelling and waving, apparently undaunted by the disaster. So, to the rapidly fading sounds of their cheers and shouts of encouragement, our fleet steadily made its way to France, pushed on by that fair wind.

12th – 16th August 1415

Like many of the vessels in our fleet, the boat that carried us to France had three huge sails and a small wooden fortress at each end of its main deck. While archers stood guard on these fore and aft "castles" as they're called, their bows at the ready, the rest of us were packed on the windswept main deck even more tightly than I have seen the sheep in their carts on market day. And this is where we remained for the entire voyage, packed like beasts being sent for slaughter, eating, sleeping and relieving our bowels and bladders as best we could. Occasionally the last of those activities caused great amusement, as when Owen Bowen attempted to pass water into the sea. Completely misjudging the wind direction, he ended up receiving a short and unpleasant shower for his troubles.

We were at sea for three whole days and the constant rocking motion of our boat caused my stomach to heave the whole time. So, along with dozens of my Welsh comrades, I spent much of the voyage hanging over the side of our boat, retching and groaning, then spewing noisily into the water below. Fortunately, this was the worst of my troubles and otherwise the trip passed without more serious mishap. At one point, though, a tethered cow on a boat quite near to us broke its rope and leaped into the sea. The poor beast bobbed about in the waves for a while before some sailors rowed a small boat to it and lashed ropes about its middle. After lots of bellowing from the cow and some energetic tugging by the men on the ship, the beast was finally hauled back aboard, to cheers from us all.

Then, during the afternoon of 14th August, just when I was thinking I could take no more of being so cruelly pitched and tossed on the endless waves, I heard the ships' lookouts cry, "Land ahoy!" Minutes later, I saw a long greenish-grey smudge on the horizon. As the brisk wind brought us nearer to it, the smudge slowly turned into rolling hills, stretches of woodland and patchwork fields, all above chalk-white cliffs. Realizing that I would soon be setting foot on this unknown shore, a feeling of excitement seized my whole being and my heart began to pound like an armourer's hammer. I wondered what beasts and men, or even what devils, I might meet in this mysterious place.

"So *that* is France," I said to my companions, in what I hoped sounded like a jaunty and devil-may-care manner, as we shielded our eyes and peered at the country we were about to invade. "Well, to me, it looks more or less like the English coast we have not long left behind."

"So, Jenkin, what were you expecting?" said Wynn, laughing. "Blue trees, green hens and seven-legged cows? Next you'll be looking out for giant Frenchmen with teeth the size of axe-heads who will come bounding through the waves and take bites from our ships!"

As I was still trying to imagine what a real Frenchman might look like, our barge passed below the chalk cliffs, then made its way into a large river estuary. On the shore to the north of us we saw a small port and, close by it, a church, houses and barns.

"What place is this?" I called to a sailor who clung to the rigging above us.

"The river is the Seine, the port is Leure and the village is St Denis," cried the sailor. "Some three miles up the estuary is the town they call Harfleur, which the King believes to be rightfully his. It seems he has chosen to claim it as the first prize in his campaign."

As I gazed at the distant shore, knowing that

hundreds of French eyes would be anxiously watching our mighty fleet enter their waters, the wind briefly changed direction and I smelled a most terrible stench, a strong sweet-sour smell, partly like decaying vegetation and partly like fish rotting on a hot summer's day.

"What awful stink is that?" I shouted to the sailor.

"Surely it can't be Frenchmen!" cried Owen. "I'd heard they never wash but this stench is far stronger than even a *thousand* putrid Frenchmen could make!"

"No!" laughed the sailor. "The smell is coming from the marshes at Harfleur. And I think that you will soon become very accustomed to it!"

Bright and early on the morning of 15th August, we began our invasion. As great white gulls screeched and the early morning sun flashed and sparkled on the waves, we gathered our weapons, climbed from our barge and squeezed into the small rowing boat that would take us on the last part of our journey to land. Soon, all around us, the sea bobbed with hundreds of similar boats, crammed with fighting-men being ferried towards the long stony beach. Protecting my eyes from the rapidly rising sun, I squinted towards it, anxious for a glimpse of my first real Frenchman. I was disappointed. Apart from rocks, it appeared empty.

"Where are the French?" cried Owen Bowen, as he too surveyed the shingle. "Do they not wish to protect their land? Why do they not rush to greet us with fire and steel?"

"They will," grunted Wynn Vaughn. "Sooner or later they will. But for the time being I think our King's choice of landing place may have caught them unawares. I believe they may have been expecting us to land further north than this."

As we neared the shoreline, I absent-mindedly watched the silver fish that darted about us, lost in thoughts of the adventures that lay ahead. Suddenly I felt a bump and heard the boat's bottom grinding on pebbles.

"Out, boys!" said Wynn. "This is it! We have arrived at the land we are to conquer. So put French soil beneath your feet and make all haste!"

Clutching our bows and packs, my companions and I scrambled from the boat, then splashed through the shallows, joining the archers who had already landed. Soon the whole beach was thronged with men, the air resounding with the shouts of our commanders.

All at once I was aware of a great excitement amongst our assembled company and I saw that everyone was staring at a large and magnificently decorated barge which had recently put out from the royal flagship and which was being beached some yards distant from us.

"It is the King!" I head someone mutter. My heart skipped a beat as I saw an athletic and richly robed figure spring confidently from the boat, then fall to his knees on the sand and raise his hands in prayer. I suddenly realized that I was looking at the 27-year-old monarch I had been so desperate to set eyes upon since the day I'd first been told of this great adventure. Far from being disappointed with my first sight of the man who would lead us into battle, I was awestruck. Henry V was every inch the glorious leader and noble hero that I had hoped he might be.

Various squires were taking turns to throw themselves at our King's feet and, as I watched him lightly touch their shoulders with his sword, I recalled what my mother had said of this monarch's legendary courage, intelligence and daring. And now, as our King stood in all his magnificence, just a few dozen paces from me, I knew that if he commanded me to do so, I would follow him to the ends of the earth and die in his cause, as it was both his and God's will that I do so.

The King began to confer with his assembled

nobles, busily studying the charts and maps which were being brought to them by various royal officials. While they did, a second royal barge arrived at the beach. Royal servants and baggage boys leaped from it and began unloading enormous wooden chests whilst others laid out great heaps of brightly coloured cloth and poles upon the sand.

"See, boys," said Wynn. "Those chests contain the King's wardrobe and bedding and the linen which will grace his royal dinner table. And the piles of canvas are the splendid royal pavilions in which he and his nobles are to spend their nights and from which the monarch will direct our campaign."

"Ha! If only we had such fine shelter!" Owen whispered. "I guarantee I would fight *twice* as well!"

"*You* are a common archer, Owen Bowen!" said Wynn. "Your roof will be the sky and your feather bed the earth beneath you. At best, and if you are *very* lucky, you may get to spend the occasional night in a leaky pigsty."

"But pigs are choosy about the company they keep," said Morgan, with a laugh. "They would run a mile if they knew they had to spend their nights with my brother. His night-time noises would offend the most piggish of swine and his snores are loud enough to wake the dead!" At this, Owen snorted loudly then gave his twin a push which sent him sprawling onto the wet sand.

"Watch yourselves, lads!" growled Wynn, as Morgan made to grab his brother's ankles. "Serious business is at hand. Your horseplay will not please our betters!"

It was time for us to move. The King and his nobles mounted the horses that had been brought up by their squires, then moved off down the beach. A moment later our captains yelled their commands and we assembled ourselves into three long columns and began to tramp towards the distant dunes. We hadn't gone far when we came upon a trench bordered by a sandbank. It presented no real obstacle but it did tell us that we weren't entirely unexpected.

"Ha!" laughed Owen, as he crossed the trench, then scrambled up the sandbank. "Is this the best they can do to protect their homeland? If it is I think we might be in Paris before the night has fallen!"

"Bonehead Bowen!" muttered Wynn. "Paris is many days' march away, boy! And we have yet to take Harfleur. Do not think the citizens will welcome us with open arms. Your head may be full of nonsense but be assured, young pudding-brain, they will still be anxious to have it on a spike. So stay watchful! A French bowman could have you in his sights this very moment."

I laughed at this, but I also looked nervously about me. As I did, I caught sight of movement some distance away. About two good arrow shots beyond us I spied a cluster of poor-looking thatched cottages. Figures scurried about, plainly in some state of alarm. As we drew nearer, I saw that some pushed handcarts while others frantically waved their arms at running cattle, which were obviously as panic-stricken as they were. It was plain to see that this wasn't an attacking French army. Whoever it was, they were getting away from us as quickly they could.

"Local farming folk fleeing King Henry's army," laughed Wynn. "What a surprise they must have had. To see such a host of ships and fighting-men in these places that are normally home to just crabs and cattle!"

If any of the French peasants had been brave enough to linger, they would probably have been even more surprised by what followed. Having ensured that the beach was entirely free of enemy forces, we returned to the boats and began the huge task of unloading our horses, supplies and weapons. My job, along with the rest of our squad, was to carry the leather buckets that contained our sheaves of arrows. There were tens of hundreds of these and, after a short time, I was soaked with sweat from the effort of carrying them from ship to shore in the midday heat. Soon, as a result of our army's labours, whole sections of the beach were littered with sheaves of arrows, siege engines, heaps of armour and cannon. There were huge piles of timber that would be used to build the hinged screens that were intended to protect our gunners when they finally launched their assault on Harfleur. Further down the shoreline, vast mountains of food, clothing and ever-lengthening lines of skittish warhorses covered almost every inch of sand.

17th – 19th August 1415

The enormous business of unloading our food and equipment took three whole days. Partway through the operation, our own company of archers received orders to join an outpost of men who were positioned between the beach and Harfleur to guard against a surprise attack from the French. In order to do this we first had to cross those foul marshes we'd smelled from our barge. We hoped to do it as quickly as possible but, as we squelched our way across the stinking mud, the captain in charge of our party spotted a bed of shellfish in one of the swamp's brackish pools. He decided that he'd like to supplement his rations with fresh seafood. Finding the shellfish to be both large and plentiful he was quickly joined by a large group of archers, including myself and Evan Lewis. Despite scornful remarks from Wynn and the Bowens about eating "nothing but sea-dwelling slugs and snails", the two of us were soon up to our knees in the foul water, greedily plucking cockles and mussels from the slime-covered rocks.

After finally crossing the marsh we reached the wooded hills where the advance guard were camped. At the summit, we got our first proper view of Harfleur. And what a lovely place the town was! I had never seen anything quite like it in my whole life and, as we gazed down upon it, I marvelled that anyone could imagine or build anything so magnificent! The whole town was completely surrounded by a curved wall surmounted with twenty or more tall and elegant towers. Each one was decorated with lovely figures painted in blue and gold which glittered in the bright sunlight: here on one, a fierce lion, on another, a huge stag, and on another, a fiery dragon. Beyond the outer edge of this wall lay a wide moat from which, as we would later discover, protruded sharpened stakes. They were there to prevent invaders like us from crossing in boats.

"The French have built a beautiful town here at Harfleur," said Morgan. "It's a pity that it will soon be destroyed when London, the King's Daughter and the Messenger begin to roar their challenges."

"It *is* a lovely town," said Wynn. "And a well-fortified one. At our briefing this morning Davy Gam warned his commanders that this place will be no easy prize. There are just three gateways, and each may only be reached by a drawbridge which in turn is guarded by massive fortifications on the other side of the moat. The French know they are well defended and will fight like demons to stop us taking their town."

We set about making our camp on the hilltop. As I laid out my equipment I occasionally cast a glance at the place we would soon attack. I knew that on the other side of those walls there would be boys just like myself looking out at us, the enemy who had appeared so suddenly on the hill opposite their town. Boys who knew that they would soon be doing their utmost to kill the foreign invaders.

Once our camp was set up, we boys were given our daily duties: digging toilet trenches, collecting firewood and fetching food and water for our men and horses.

"Are we ever going to get to fight the Frenchies?" Morgan said in frustration as we lugged yet more water buckets up the hillside from the stream below our camp. "Or are we to spend all our days being errand boys and feeders of horses?"

"You'll get your chance for action soon enough," said Wynn. "And when it does come you may well wish you were still carrying buckets of water!"

The following afternoon, the last of our supplies and equipment were finally brought up from the boats and the King's engineers and labourers began setting up our cannon and siege machines around Harfleur. It was while this difficult and dangerous task was being carried out that the French, who had so far remained hidden behind their walls, made their first attack on our forces.

It happened while the Bowens and I were collecting firewood on a hillside a few hundred yards from our camp. Taking a brief rest from our task, we had paused to watch a group of English gunners and labourers who were working in the valley below us. All of them were busily pulling on ropes and heaving massive levers as they attempted to shift one of the huge cannon into place. As they struggled and sweated under the hot August sun, one of them suddenly fell to his knees, then slumped forward, flat on his face. At first, we thought he'd collapsed from the strain of his task, or from heat exhaustion. But then I saw that there was a crossbow bolt sticking out of his neck.

"Look!" I gasped. "The poor fellow's been shot!"

"We must do something!" cried Morgan, desperately looking around for his bow.

"But what?" said Owen. "We're here to collect firewood. We cannot act alone. Our orders must first come from Wynn or Davy Gam."

Before any of us could say or do another thing we heard a whistling sound and saw a second bolt thud into the man's back. He twitched a couple of times, then lay still. Realizing they were under attack, the man's companions had thrown down their tools and ropes and were racing for the protection of the nearest trees. Not quickly enough though, for as they scrambled for cover a whole series of crossbow bolts began to spew from the slits in Harfleur's towers. Soon, four more men also lay twitching with half a dozen crossbow bolts protruding from their backs.

Rendered immobile by shock and fear, we watched this whole scene in stunned silence. Apart from those poor souls I had seen perish on the blazing ships and the one occasion when I had seen a childhood playmate crushed under the wheels of a hay cart, it was my first experience of seeing anyone die such a violent death. It left me pale and shaken for the rest of that day. I think it had finally dawned on me that injury and death were going to be my constant companions for all of the coming weeks and months.

When King Henry heard of the attack on his gunners and labourers he was greatly troubled. Realizing that they were now so dangerously exposed to the French defenders, he immediately ordered his carpenters to speed up the construction of the protective wooden screens. This move didn't come a moment too soon. Not only did bolts from the French crossbowmen in the towers begin to fly towards our men more and more often, but up on the town walls the French cannon had also begun to roar their defiance. They were frequently hurling great blasts of shot towards our positions. Alongside them, more ancient missile launchers also lobbed lethal loads of stone and shale.

Encouraged by their successful attacks on our forces, it wasn't long before the French began to try a new tactic to prevent us setting up our siege engines and cannon. And it was during one of these assaults that I actually got a proper sight of my first real Frenchmen. I was busy loading sheaves of arrows into leather buckets when I became aware that a barrage of cannon and crossbow fire had erupted from the walls of

Harfleur. A second later the town gates were flung open and I saw a whole mob of men come dashing out of them, yelling and screaming for all they were worth and firing arrows as they ran. These French soldiers, who, as far as I could tell, looked more or less like normal men, were headed straight for the labourers working on our gun positions. Before our astonished men had time to react, the French pounced on six or seven of them and began hauling them back towards Harfleur. They dragged them into the town and the gates were closed behind them. Blood-curdling screams could soon be heard coming from somewhere behind the town walls. It was clear that the unfortunate kidnapped workers were being tortured or killed by the French.

Just then my comrades dashed up to me. I noticed that they were all clutching their bows and quivers full of arrows.

"Jenkin!" yelled Wynn. "You can prove yourself worthy of your six pence a day. Davy Gam has commanded us to join the archers giving cover to the labourers. He is expecting more surprise attacks from the French at any moment. Fetch your bow! We are to report to the wooden barricade down by the Messenger!"

"Do as the man says, Jenkin!" cried Owen. "At last we have our chance for action!"

I was suddenly beset by a strange mixture of dread and excitement, but uppermost in my thoughts was my promise to my father. I would prove myself worthy of his trust and of the magnificent weapon he had bestowed upon me. With this in mind I grabbed my bow and sheaf of arrows, crouched low, then sprinted after my friends who were already dashing in the direction of the distant barricade.

When we reached it we found Davy Gam and his archers squatting behind it. At Davy's command I notched an arrow to my bowstring and prepared myself for the next French attack.

Half an hour later no such attack had come. But the Messenger was ready for action.

"See, boys!" said Evan Lewis excitedly. "We have done our bit. Now the Frenchies will tremble in their boots!"

Protected by the wooden screens, the gunners carried out their final preparations. Such was the size of the gun that no less than ten men were busily priming it in readiness for firing, whilst another ten staggered towards the barrel, completely dwarfed by the enormous stone cannonball they were struggling to support.

"I'd put your fingers in your ears if I were you, my archer boys," cried Davy Gam, as they finally dropped the ball into the Messenger's mouth. "This gun's messages are of the sort that destroy eardrums as well as stone walls."

I did as Davy said, and only just in time. Seconds later, the wooden screen was raised and the master gunner put his flaming torch to the Messenger's breech. Suddenly, there was an almighty brain-rattling roar, and clouds of choking, black smoke and red and orange flames belched from the Messenger's mouth. At the same time, the giant gun jerked wildly on its platform and all of the gunners were thrown into the air, then engulfed by smoke.

As the smoke began to clear I saw that they were all sprawled on the ground, some of them seemingly dead. But after a few moments they began to drag themselves to their feet, looking dazed and bewildered, but otherwise uninjured. Such was the force of the explosion that it had knocked every single one of them flat on their backs! But their efforts hadn't been for nothing. As the smoke cleared further I could plainly make out the huge, ragged hole which the Messenger's giant cannonball had punched in Harfleur's wall. Along with my excited comrades, I immediately leaped to my feet and gave a great cheer.

"Would you look at that!" cried Evan. "These Frenchies don't waste a moment!"

I could hardly believe my eyes. As fragments of stone cascaded from the battlements and my ears still rang with the noise of the explosion, a crowd of French soldiers and builders were frantically clambering into the enormous breach in Harfleur's shattered wall. They immediately set to work, filling it with stones and wood. They worked at such speed that it looked as though the damage would be repaired in no time. But Davy Gam commanded us to open fire on the repair gang, and one second later, I shot my first arrow at a Frenchman.

It was the first of hundreds, possibly even tens of hundreds, that I would fire in the coming days and months. Such was my excitement and so violently did my hands tremble that I am ashamed to say it missed. So did my next, and my next, but when I shot my fourth I think I may have been somewhat calmer and more settled to my task, for I saw my shaft thud into the forearm of one of the enemy as he bent to pick up a large stone. He clutched desperately at the arrow and dropped his stone.

"They're sitting ducks!" cried Owen excitedly, as he notched a shaft to his own bow. "They don't stand a chance, do they, Jenkin?"

I grinned, believing he spoke the truth, and drew back my bowstring to fire once more. But we hadn't reckoned with the French soldiers who were rapidly taking their positions on the walls above us. As I sighted my arrow on my next target, I heard a yell of pain and turned to see that a crossbow bolt had embedded itself in the neck of a boy just a few yards away from me. He'd toppled backwards into the dirt, squirming in agony as blood bubbled from his wounds. I looked up and saw that a long line of French crossbowmen had us in their sights and were loosing one bolt after another in our direction. In their elevated position the Frenchmen were perfectly placed to pick us off. Then their cannon joined in this ferocious assault and a hail of rock and shale showered down on us. The tables were turned. We were the sitting ducks.

Huge chunks of rock and jagged stone began bouncing off the ground all around me and arrows thudded into our barricade and my fellow archers. I was gripped by a bowel-wrenching panic of a kind I'd never felt before in my entire life. I was as helpless and

terrified as a rabbit in a snare. Then the truth hit me –
I might possibly perish in this, my first encounter with
the enemy!

Quite soon, some twenty of our archers lay dead in
the dust, while a dozen more groaned in pain from
horrific stone and crossbow wounds. And then, I saw
our own Owen Bowen throw his arms in the air, spin
round, and sprawl on the ground beside me.

I felt a strong arm grasp my shoulder and turned to
see Wynn, looking grim-faced and pointing to the
French above us. "It's no good, Jenkin!" he yelled, as
the French cannon roared and roared again. "They
have us at their mercy. We must withdraw!"

"But what about my brother?" cried Morgan,
pointing to Owen, who lay in the dirt moaning pitifully
and clutching his head.

"We must first retreat, then get him to the surgeons'
tents with all speed!" barked Wynn.

Morgan and I helped Owen to his feet. With his
arms draped round our shoulders, we staggered out
from behind the barricade, our heads bent low to
avoid the onslaught. Harry, Evan and Wynn attempted
to give us covering fire. We were quickly followed by a
dozen more archers, some of them also carrying and
dragging wounded comrades. With crossbow bolts

whistling round our ears and cannon smoke stinging our eyes and burning our throats, we retreated, staggering this way and that as we struggled to support Owen's enormous weight.

We eventually reached the surgeons' tents where we laid our wounded comrade on a straw-covered bench. Owen had been struck on the head by pieces of stone from the French cannon and blood was pouring from two large gashes on his nose and forehead.

"My tenth today," said the surgeon, as he wiped Owen's wounds with a filthy rag. "You walking wounded are becoming more common as each hour passes."

As he tended our injured friend I gazed around the tent. Everywhere I looked I saw blankets and straw-filled mattresses laid out in readiness for the wounded and sick who would no doubt soon be arriving in ever-increasing numbers. There were already a few unfortunate souls stretched out on these makeshift beds. Some just groaned quietly to themselves but others thrashed about wildly, obviously in torment from the agony of their terrible wounds. Some, an awful ghostly white colour, lay completely still, staring up at the canvas ceiling. For all I knew, they might already have been dead. Close by, I saw the equipment and supplies which the surgeons relied upon to ease suffering and save lives. There were rolls of bandages, pots of ointments made from flowers, sacks filled with herbs, and jars brimming with the squirming leeches the surgeons would press to the flesh of those who needed to be bled.

"Just cuts and bruises," said the surgeon, as he finished examining Owen's head. "You'll live to fight another day."

He plunged his hand into a large jar of sweet-smelling ointment and began smearing it on Owen's wounds, saying, "You'll have a headache, but you'll be fine to go back to the front line in a day or so."

"I think I feel a bit better already," Owen said quietly, while the surgeon began wrapping a bandage round his head.

"And you smell just like a spring meadow in Tregarth!" joked Harry as we finally helped Owen up from the bench.

"Well, that makes a change from his usual cesspit stink!" laughed Morgan, obviously feeling very relieved to discover that his beloved brother's wounds were only minor ones.

As we left the tent with our injured comrade, I spotted a large box filled with knives and saws. "Are they what I think they're for?" I asked Wynn.

"Yes, they are," he said, confirming my worst fears. "But let's hope those sawbones don't have to use those blades on *your* broken and mangled bodies, my fine young archer boys," he growled. "And if they do, pray it's not your arms or hands they hack off!"

Within a few days of our bloody encounter with the French archers all of our cannon and siege machines were finally ready. Now our army's great onslaught on Harfleur could begin in earnest. Soon, giant stone balls, shot and entire millstones began to crash into the walls of the town both day and night, while flocks of arrows and crossbow bolts constantly flew back and forth between our own positions and the French archers on the towers and ramparts. I began to feel as though there had never been any time in my entire life when my ears hadn't rung to the sound of deafening explosions and the screams of dying and wounded men; when my nostrils and throat had been free of the smell and taste of that thick cannon smoke. And of course, we also had to endure the sickening stench of those reeking Harfleur marshes.

Under the non-stop pounding from our weapons, huge sections of Harfleur's walls began to topple into the streets of the town. Later, I would discover the terrible damage this inflicted on Harfleur's citizens and soldiers. Some of our missiles, wrapped in flaming, pitch-soaked rags, would fall onto the town's wooden buildings, instantly setting them ablaze. From outside the town's walls I would hear the crackle of burning timber as one of these incendiaries hit its target, then see clouds of smoke billowing up above the walls as flames began to sweep through whole rows of wooden houses.

Within days Harfleur was no longer the pretty town I had first set eyes upon from that wooded hilltop. Ragged holes gaped in its walls, plumes of smoke drifted across its ruined battlements and many of its lovely towers were no more than blackened, smouldering stumps. However, despite the damage we inflicted upon them and their town, the French continued to defend with unceasing daring and energy. It was still too dangerous for us to get really close to the walls with the battering rams which would break down doors and wooden ramparts, and with the siege towers from which we would hurl missiles into the town.

One morning, about six days into the siege, I spied a large group of our soldiers dashing towards Harfleur's ramparts with the siege ladder with which they intended to scale the town wall. But they had barely got the ladder against it when a group of Frenchmen appeared above them, carrying a cauldron which they tipped in the direction of our soldiers. The men on and below the ladder were instantly engulfed in a dark, bubbling, hissing liquid that spat and steamed. Alongside the shouts of joy and delight from the French, our comrades' screams of pain rang out so loudly and so terribly, that I feared they could be heard across the English Channel.

"Boiling oil," said Wynn, as I watched the reddened and scalded survivors staggering back to our lines. "'Twill have seared the flesh from those poor men's bones."

As if all the noise and death and injury that was around me every day wasn't torment enough, the weather began to grow hotter. As each day passed, the sun blazed down with increasing ferocity and soon, after carrying out even the smallest action, I was drenched in sweat and gasping for breath.

"Things could be worse," said Harry one day, pointing to a group of our knights, all of them encased from head to toe in armour. "We could be like them, trapped inside their metal ovens."

The ever-increasing heat brought new problems. Swarms of biting flies rose from the Harfleur swamps and our own toilet pits. They buzzed around us the whole day long, driving both men and horses to the point of madness. As the days went by I began to feel as though I'd had all my thoughts of glory, excitement and adventure in some other life.

Just when it seemed like things couldn't possibly get any worse, they did. About eight or nine days into the siege I was making my way to the latrine pits, having been feeling hot and sickly for some hours. My stomach was suddenly gripped by the most terrible, agonizing cramps and such was my pain that I doubled up instantly and was soon sprawled across the baked earth, clutching my gut and groaning and shuddering in turns. I soiled my breeches, being quite unable to control the movements of my bowels. As I lay there, wondering what terrible affliction I was suffering, I felt a comforting hand upon my shoulder and I looked up to see that it belonged to a small and shifty-looking archer boy, a few years older than me.

"You don't look too good!" said the boy. "I reckon

you must have an attack of the bloody flux. They say it's been getting a real grip round here these last few days."

He then took a dirty rag from his tunic and wiped away the cold beads of sweat that were covering my brow, saying, "Don't you worry, chum. I'll get you to the surgeon's tent. They'll soon have you feeling right as rain!" and with that he hoisted me from the ground and put my arm round his shoulder.

"By the way, mate," he said, as we made our way through the camp, "my name's Tobias Simcock and I'm from Malden, in the county of Kent. What's yours?"

"Jenkin Lloyd," I said. "I'm from Wales. I'm with a group of archers who were enlisted from my home village of Tregarth."

"Well," laughed Tobias, "joining King Henry's army wasn't quite that simple with me. I was sort of given an offer I couldn't refuse. After a little problem with some cheese that went missing from a market stall, if you know what I mean." He winked, then added, "I was given a choice. Either I joined up or spent the rest of my days in clink."

"Oh yes, I see," I said. I remembered Wynn saying that hundreds of the archers in the King's army were prisoners who'd been pardoned on condition that they fought in France.

"Now tell me, Jenkin," said Tobias. "You by any chance been sampling them cockles and whatnot from down in them horrid, stinking marshes?"

"Yes, I have," I groaned. "We collected some not long after landing. And yesterday some men from our unit slipped away and fetched some more. We ate them last night."

"What!" Tobias laughed. "The men … or the cockles?" Then he looked serious and said, "I got bad news for you, mate. All the human muck and whatnot from Harfleur's latrines flows into them marshes. And it settles at the very spot where the shellfish are in their greatest numbers. That's why they're all so big an' fat an' juicy!"

As Tobias said this another crippling wave of sickness seized my insides and I once more began to retch.

"But then again," said Tobias, when my spasm had finally passed, "it could have just as well have been the green apples from the orchards in the valley. A couple of blokes in my unit ate a sackful and now they've got the bloody flux an' all! And then there's the wine our lads have been looting from the French farms round here. Sour as vinegar, but they guzzle it like they was blinkin' fish out of water. All sorts of rotten grub can bring on the bloody flux." He grinned, then said, "Now me, I prefer proper vittles and drink. Good English roast beef and ale. Fresh eggs. Fine wines. Mutton. You'd be amazed how many store-tent flaps and whatnot get left open round these parts. Seems only right that someone pops in and rescues all that good grub before the thieves can snaffle it!"

Finally we reached the surgeons' tents and Tobias said, "Right, Jenkin, mate! Here you are. I'll be off now. Don't you worry. I'll pop by in a few days and see how you're doin'!"

Before I'd time to thank him he'd slipped away as quickly as he'd appeared. I made my way into the nearest tent to discover that, in addition to the men and boys who'd been wounded in battle, it was also filling up with men and boys in a similar state to myself.

"Another one!" said the surgeon, as I told him of my plight. "What was it with you? Shellfish? Rotgut wine?" Then, before I could answer, he frowned and said, "Right! Let's get you to a bed!"

He led me to a pile of straw and blankets and left me there. I collapsed in a pathetic, shuddering heap, chilled to the marrow, soaked in sweat, my head spinning and my stomach heaving twenty times more violently than it had done when we were at sea. I was sure I would die at any moment.

Some hours later the Bowen twins entered the sick tent. Between them they were supporting Evan Lewis, who looked as if he was in an even worse state than I was. After they'd handed him over to the surgeons they came to my bedside and Owen said, "This'll teach you to eat sea-slugs!" Then he looked grave and said, "But seriously, Jenkin, we wish you a speedy recovery. Each night we'll pray to God that you both live to fight another day."

For the next three days I lay on my sickbed, sipping the infusions of herbs the surgeons gave me and listening to the moans and groans of the sick and dying men who filled the tents in ever-increasing numbers. I felt dreadful but I was one of the lucky ones. My own case of the bloody flux turned out to be far less serious than that of many unfortunate souls around me. After a few days I began to feel well enough to eat a little bread and gruel. On my fourth day in the surgeons' tent, Tobias Simcock, true to his word, paid me a visit.

"Well, Jenkin, mate," he said, "you look ten times better than last time I saw you." As he spoke, I noticed that his tunic had a strange bulge in it. Seeing my puzzled expression, he grinned, then reached inside his tunic and took out a cloth-wrapped bundle, saying, "Here, mate. Cold roast chicken and beef. And a loaf and cheese. And some beer!" Then he winked and said, "But don't ask where it all came from!" And with that he left again, saying that we might not meet again for some time as his unit was due to move to the east of Harfleur, where they were to give covering fire to the siege machines.

A couple of days after this the surgeons pronounced me fit enough to take up my duties again and, although I was still occasionally troubled by sudden loose-bowel attacks, I was soon back at my siege post and once more firing my arrows at the French. But it was not to be so for Evan and hundreds more like him. During the following days the bloody flux tightened its terrible grip on our army. Soon it became impossible to move around the camp without coming on groaning men squatting behind tents, trees and wagons, their hose round their ankles, as they strained to relieve their agony, unable to reach the latrines in time. Almost overnight our camp appeared to transform itself into one great, stinking toilet pit. The surgeons' tents were full to overflowing, and all around the camp men were curled up like babies, hugging their knees to their chests and moaning with pain, as the air about them grew more foul by the moment. The doctors worked ceaselessly, giving the sick herbal remedies, applying leeches to their flesh and putting razors to their veins, letting their blood gush forth to let out poisonous vapours. Nevertheless, in spite of the doctors' work and the ceaseless praying of our priests, it wasn't long before the flux victims began to die and soon groups of labourers were hard at work digging a massive pit in which to bury the ever-growing heaps of bodies.

The nobles were not spared this terrible affliction either. The King's own brother was struck down, and so was the Bishop of Norwich. After five days of agonized suffering the Bishop died, causing much unhappiness to our King, who had loved him dearly.

"It's a blessing for them," said Owen, as he and I watched the men carry yet another batch of corpses to the burial pit at the edge of the stinking marsh. "At least their suffering is finally over."

Fortunately, Evan Lewis's suffering did not end in one of those burial pits. After some days he began to recover and was transferred to the tents where the flux survivors rested after their illness. However, he was still far too weak to resume his archer's duties.

Throughout this terrible time of disease and death, our bombardment of Harfleur continued. All those men and boys who were fit and weren't tending the sick or carrying the dead to the grave pits were constantly engaged in the attack on the town. But then we discovered that, just like so many of our own soldiers, the citizens of Harfleur were also suffering and dying from the bloody flux.

"Surely they must surrender now," said Morgan Bowen, as we watched flames lick around the fortified town entrance they called the Leure Gate. "For weeks now we've prevented food and supplies from reaching them, we've bombarded and burned their town, and now they are gripped by the bloody flux. It must be more than they can endure."

"They are obviously hanging on in the hope that their king and nobles will come to their rescue," said Harry.

"But they've been doing that for weeks!" I said. "And still no reinforcements have arrived. I think that if I were a citizen of Harfleur I would be thinking I had been deserted by my King. And by his heir, the Dauphin."

"And you'd probably be right," said Wynn. "King Charles VI of France is of little use to his people. By all reports he is half mad and thinks himself made of glass. He is so afraid that he will smash into a thousand pieces that he frequently won't let anyone near him. And as for the Dauphin and the French nobles of his court, they are so busy squabbling that it would be a miracle if they united in the defence of their land. I really do think there is no hope for Harfleur."

Nevertheless, even though Harfleur's brave defenders seemed to have been abandoned by their monarch, they continued to put up a ferocious resistance, launching ever more reckless attacks on our guns. One particular day, myself, Harry and the Bowen twins were in a group of 30 archers commanded by Davy Gam. We were in front of a line of wagons stacked with casks. They contained the gunpowder being used by the smoke-blackened gunners who fired the King's Daughter – we were there to give them cover. Suddenly a squadron of French soldiers came racing from a gap in the damaged town wall, all of them screaming like lunatics.

Our first volley of arrows brought down eight of them while another six just turned and ran. But a hard core of about ten kept coming at us. They were led by a big, mad-looking fellow who, despite being hit by three or four arrows in both his neck and thighs, continued to race towards us, his face contorted in agony and his eyes blazing with hatred. All of our attackers were carrying burning torches and, as they neared us, they hurled them, yelling loudly. I think it must have been the big fellow's which hit the supply wagons.

There was a massive explosion and pieces of jagged wood, metal and chunks of earth began to rain down on everyone. What followed is a bit of a blur, but I do remember that there was some vicious hand-to-hand fighting before I ended up on the ground with the big, mad-looking Frenchman on top of me. I think that if brave Davy Gam hadn't come to my aid, my attacker would have had the better of me, but our little Welsh leader laid into him so ferociously that I believe even a full-grown ox wouldn't have survived his onslaught. Soon the man lay lifeless at Davy's feet. Apart from receiving some painful bruising about my face and chest and two deep and bloody cuts on my neck, I was otherwise unharmed. After having my wounds bandaged by Wynn I shakily rose to my feet and attempted to gather my wits.

Just after this we found Harry. He was lying face down, and embedded in his back was a large piece of jagged metal, possibly part of an iron band from a cartwheel. His head was twisted awkwardly to one side and his eyes had a strange misty look to them. As he lay there, shivering and groaning, his fingers clawing desperately at the earth, he attempted to raise himself on his hands and knees. It was then that we saw that the jagged metal had passed right through him.

"I think I'm dying," he said, turning his head and giving us a look I'll never forget. "I wish my ma were here to make me better. Tell her I love her, will you?" And then he slumped down again.

Morgan and I simply stood and looked at him in stunned silence but Wynn gently placed his hand on the part of his neck where his pulse would be.

"He's gone," he said, staring up at us with an expression of absolute disbelief. "Harry's dead."

Numb and shocked at the death of this person who had been my friend and companion for as long as I could remember, I helped the others carry Harry's shattered and bloody body back to the camp. Then, after some searching, we found a priest to say the last rites over him. This done, we took him to the pit on the edge of the marshes and laid him alongside all the other hundreds of boys and men who had died from the bloody flux and the wounds they'd received in battle. And then we returned to our camp.

While the cannon continued to pound Harfleur and the flames of blazing buildings lit up the night sky, I set about greasing my bowstring and stocking up on new arrows in preparation for the next day's conflict. And that was when the tears of anguish and grief began to stream down my face. I finally realized I'd never see my cousin, dear Harry, again, and never again hear his cheery voice cry, "Good shot, Jenkin!" at our village butts.

The next morning, my heart heavy with sorrow, I returned to our siege point, wondering if I might be the next to go to the grave pits. But then, as I positioned myself behind our barricade, I saw something that caused my spirits to lift a little, despite my terrible grief. During the night, the King's Daughter had been dragged even closer to the walls of Harfleur, and many more holes had appeared in the town's defences. So many in fact, that I could clearly see French soldiers and townsfolk scurrying amongst the piles of smoking rubble that littered their ruined streets. Then, later that morning, we were told that the fortifications defending the Leure Gate had collapsed completely. Wynn informed us that the King had sent his Herald to the French, demanding their surrender, and was awaiting their reply. It looked as though the nightmare of our siege of Harfleur might finally be nearing its end.

But it wasn't to be, not just yet. The French sent the King's Herald back, refusing his demands. This was the signal for us to recommence our attack with renewed fury. King Henry ordered that every weapon and every man at his disposal be used in one final all-out assault. We fired volley after volley of arrows into Harfleur while our knights, and even sailors from our fleet, built wooden bridges across the moat, set up ladders at the walls and pounded at wood and stonework with massive battering rams. Meanwhile, our cannon continued to hurl balls and millstones, reducing even more houses to rubble and sending great chunks of stone from the church's steeple crashing into the streets below. To the east, our siege catapults battered stricken walls and buildings with yet more rocks and boulders.

Our relentless onslaught continued all through that

day and night with ever-increasing ferocity and great loss of life on both sides. But then, as dawn broke, a French messenger stepped out of the smoking rubble and approached our leaders.

Half an hour later our guns fell silent and, for the first time in weeks, my ears didn't ring to the sound of explosions and the ground beneath my feet didn't shake and tremble.

"What news?" I asked, as Wynn returned from speaking with our captain.

"A truce has been called," said Wynn. "The French have asked for five days' peace. If help hasn't arrived before then they will surrender."

For five days the crash of cannon fire and the crunch of shot slamming into stonework was absent from my life. The constant din of battle was replaced by an eerie silence, occasionally broken by the whinnying of horses or the barking of dogs. And as this silence continued, it gradually became apparent to me that the help the French craved so desperately would never come. I think the battered citizens of Harfleur must have realized this too for, even though a smaller French force was gathering on the distant southern bank of the Seine, they decided they'd had enough and finally surrendered to our King.

On 22nd September 1415, Harfleur finally became ours and we entered the town. I saw for myself the destruction I had helped bring upon this once lovely place. It was a terrible sight. Everywhere I looked were smoking ruins, shattered houses, lumps of stone, piles of filth and pools of stinking sewage. And in amongst all this devastation I could see dozens and dozens of the town's dead. Some were partly buried in the rubble, an arm sticking out here, a leg there. But others were just slumped where they had fallen, killed by an arrow or lump of stone. Rats scurried this way and that, sniffing at the rotting corpses, whilst swarms of flies buzzed frantically above them, settling on the bodies for just moments, then rising in black clouds as I passed. And everywhere, almost blotting out the foul odours from the marsh, I could smell the terrible stink of death.

As we moved amongst the ruined buildings, stepping round rubble and peering into the damaged houses which were still standing, the starving and defeated citizens of Harfleur crouched in their doorways, watching us with both terror and hatred. A

Welsh archer just a few yards ahead of me pushed past an old woman who sat on her doorstep and entered her house. He soon emerged clutching two beautiful red tablecloths.

"For my ma!" he bellowed. "She'll love them!"

"It's the rules of war, boys," said Wynn, with a shrug. "Anything that can be moved is plunder."

I think that was a signal for us all. Soon, we too were entering buildings, intent on finding treasures we could take back to our homes. While the Bowens and Wynn set about helping themselves to pots, pans, rich fabrics and mirrors from a very grand-looking house overlooking the market place, I rushed into a cobbler's workshop and grabbed myself a new leather tunic and a fine pair of boots. Even though I knew that I was stealing from the wretched, defeated folk of Harfleur, I simply couldn't resist the temptation and, despite the feelings of guilt and shame that accompanied my every action, I had soon kitted myself out with a new belt and a pair of excellent leather breeches too.

As I paused to admire the effect of my new finery in Owen's mirror I suddenly remembered poor Evan back on his sickbed in the camp. Realizing that he too had played his part in our victory, I dashed into a half-ruined tavern and grabbed some pottery jugs decorated with laughing, bearded faces. Our friend would at least have something to show the people of Tregarth that he too had been at the siege of Harfleur.

Fourteen days after the siege had ended we left Harfleur. Our King and his nobles had been uncertain as to what their next move should be. The siege had taken weeks longer than the King had planned. Of the 9,000 men we had arrived with, some 2,000, including our own Evan and Harry, had been killed or were too sick to continue in the campaign. In order to secure the town the King had to leave another 1,000 men to rebuild the defences and guard against the possibility of another attack from the French. This left just 6,000 fighting-men, made up of 1,000 knights and 5,000 archers. And many of our force were in a very sorry state indeed, being both weak from illness and hunger and dressed in little more than rags.

The prospect of marching on Paris, the King's original plan, looked very risky, especially as autumn had arrived and the weather was becoming colder by the day. But the idea of simply returning to England was out of the question. The capture of one small town would hardly have seemed worth the enormous sum of money the campaign had cost so far, not to mention all the suffering and the lives which had been lost. So, having called his Council of War on 5th October, our King decided to take us northwards and pay a visit to his French town of Calais before finally sailing for home. We were to embark on a *chevauchee*, a march in which our army would leave its cannon and siege engines at Harfleur, then swiftly progress across enemy territory, generally showing contempt for our foes. But, before we set off, all of our sick and wounded comrades were to be shipped back to England. So it was with great sadness, but also great relief for our good pal, that the Bowens, Wynn and I said our farewells to Evan Lewis, giving him messages of love to pass on to our families when he finally reached Tregarth. As we waved our goodbyes, he was lifted onto the cart that would take him to the quayside where the casualties were being loaded onto ships bound for England.

It was also a relief to finally be leaving Harfleur, even though we had no idea what dangers the coming march held in store for us. At least we would finally be free of the stomach-churning stench that seeped out of the poisonous Harfleur marshes and those filthy flies that still occasionally drove us mad with their buzzing and biting, despite the onset of colder weather.

The night before our departure I slept badly and woke frequently. As I lay staring at the flickering campfires of the French forces that were still gathering on the other side of the Harfleur estuary and felt the biting autumn chill strike through my clothes, I remembered that terrible thirtieth day of the siege. I recalled how one moment my cousin, Harry Price, had been loosing his arrows at the attacking Frenchmen and how the next he had been on the ground, writhing in agony, the life gushing from him as he sobbed so pitifully and called for his ma to come and make him better. And now my pal lay cold and stiff as a winter icicle in those crowded grave pits by the reeking marsh. Then I thought of my own ma and my sister, Gwynn, and wondered whether I would ever see them again.

The next morning dawned cold and still. The whole camp was shrouded in a deathly, bone-chilling, white mist that swirled around us as we painfully dragged ourselves from the frozen earth and began to gather our weapons and belongings. The air was soon filled with the snorts of horses and the cries of carters as the great wooden wagons carrying armour and provisions began to trundle out of our encampment, their iron-clad wheels crunching and grinding across the frosted mud. Soon the whole army was on the move and I too shouldered my bow and joined my fellow archers. As we made our way to our defensive position on the army's right flank, the supplies sergeant handed each of us one loaf, one flask of wine and a hunk of salted dried pork.

"Make it last, lads," he growled cheerily. "This might be the only decent fare yer get for weeks." We all laughed, thinking he spoke in jest. But, as it turned out, he was closer to the truth than any of us ever imagined.

I can still recall the sounds and sights of that morning as vividly as though it were yesterday. The sounds of masons' hammers on stone and carpenters' axes on timber as the King's workmen set about rebuilding the beautiful little town that we, his army, had just spent four whole weeks destroying. The huge, sickly-sweet-smelling heaps of dung that lay steaming in the roadway, dropped by the massive warhorses of the knights as they plodded northwards. The harsh, unforgiving yells of the captains as some poor man or horse stumbled in a pothole, then screamed in agony, their leg broken, completely unable to move. The clouds of breath which constantly billowed from the mouths and nostrils of thousands and thousands of men and animals in the cold morning air. And the tired-looking trees at the roadside, their brown leaves fluttering steadily to the ground – another sign that our siege had gone on far longer than the King had intended and that cruel winter was on its way. I can recall it all in an instant. But one thing comes back to me more powerfully than all of these others put together. And that's the terrible feeling that lay deep in my chest as we tramped away from Harfleur. The feeling that, despite all the astonishing and terrifying things I'd seen and done so far, my great adventure was only just beginning.

On 11th October we reached the town of Arques where we were to cross the River Bethune. Massive rocky crags towered above the water here, and on top of them stood the town's castle. The bridge spanning the river was very narrow at this point so only a few men and horses could cross it at a time. As there seemed to be no sign of activity from the town or castle, our commanders signalled for the leading troops to advance and the first of our knights, foot soldiers and pack horses slowly began to make their way across.

"Looks like the French are cowering in their cellars," said Owen as we waited to cross, some 30 yards or so from the bridge. "If all the towns are like this, we'll be at Calais in no time."

At that moment there was an enormous explosion from somewhere above us and I looked up to see tongues of flame erupting from the cannon on the castle walls. An instant later, a deluge of stone shot crashed down amongst the fighting-men and wagons crossing the bridge. Horses reared and screamed, men fell to their knees and yelled in pain, while captains shouted and did their best to maintain order. When the dust and smoke finally cleared I saw that at least six men were lying in bloody crumpled heaps on the bridge's cobbles, while several more staggered around aimlessly, blood pouring from their wounds. As the casualties were carried back to the surgeons' carts, our leaders took stock of the situation. It was clear we were halted, at least for the time being.

Morgan sighed. "Now we're in a pretty pickle," he said. "They have us where they want us. We do not even have our great guns with which to return their fire."

"Don't despair, Morgan Bowen," growled Wynn. "Have faith in your King. He is not our leader for nothing! There are more ways than one to skin a cat."

And, as was so often the case, Wynn's words proved correct and our delay was brief. As we took a welcome rest by the roadside, our determined monarch sent a message to the castle-governor of Arques, telling him that if we were not given safe passage over the bridge we would burn his town and the surrounding fields and farms to the ground. Then, to make sure he realized this was no idle threat, he sent men carrying lighted torches into the meadows around the town. It had the desired effect. Not long afterwards, the castle-governor came out and told us he would grant us passage across the bridge. And that wasn't all.

"Look!" cried Owen, as our horses and troops once more began to move over the bridge. "The gates are opening. Surely they aren't going to attack us now?" But it wasn't hostile knights that came out from the town. It was wagons pulled by heavy horses. There were at least twenty of them and, as they creaked and clattered their way across the cobbles, I saw that every one was piled with flasks of wine and baskets filled with hundreds of loaves of bread.

"A gift from the castle-governor," said Wynn with a smile. "No doubt to speed us on our way. He has learned of the destruction we brought upon Harfleur and is anxious to see the last of us. If all it costs him is bread and wine, then he will be happy."

"Well, at last *some* good luck has befallen us," said Owen, as we sat by our fire later that evening, tearing off great chunks of French bread and washing them down with red wine. "Perhaps this is the beginning of better days."

The next morning it began to rain. Not a heavy downpour but a fine freezing mist that hung around and seemed to soak through my very skin. And, as well as drenching us all, the rain made marching much more difficult. The damp earth of the broken, pitted roads quickly turned to clinging mud which stuck to my shoes in clods, making my feet feel as heavy as blacksmiths' anvils. Then, just to add to our ever-increasing troubles and discomforts, Davy Gam gathered us together and told us that the King had decided that our marching pace must be quickened.

"He's realized Calais is much further than he first thought," said Davy. "He knows our food rations are almost gone and is hoping to reach safety before we starve."

"Quickening our pace is fine for knights and mounted archers!" grumbled Morgan later that same morning. "They dig in their spurs and let their horses do the rest! It's us foot-sloggers who suffer. And would you look at the state of my boots. They're falling to pieces. In fact I'm no longer sure whether my feet are shod in leather or just the foul mud from this road!"

That day we marched twenty miles and, just as the light began to fade, we reached the outskirts of the town of Eu and the bridge over the River Bresle. I was wet and exhausted, caked in mud, starving hungry and desperate to rest my aching back and legs.

Then, just when we were almost at the bridge, and for the second time in two days, we were met with a barrage of cannon shot from the town that stood in our path. And this time it wasn't just artillery that threatened us. As our leading troops milled about in confusion, the gates of Eu opened and a large force of mounted French knights suddenly galloped towards them. Before our soldiers had chance to react, the knights had charged into them, hacking and stabbing at them with swords, lances and maces. At this, a large group of our own mounted knights quickly galloped to the defence of their comrades, supported by a squad of archers. A short but fierce battle followed with men on both sides being killed and wounded, but eventually the French were overwhelmed and forced to retreat to the safety of their town walls.

So once more we found our way blocked by the cannon of a small but defiant French town and, once more, our King was obliged to make his threat to burn the local farms. And, just as it had done at Arques, the threat worked, with the townsfolk not only waving us on over their bridge, but also giving more bread and wine to help us on our way.

The next morning, after dragging ourselves from the ditches and hedge-bottoms where we had passed the night, we breakfasted on the bread and wine which the good citizens of Eu had so kindly donated to us, then continued our weary trek north. As we marched, I began to notice the toll that weeks of besieging Harfleur and trekking the muddy and potholed French roads was taking on our army's clothes and equipment. Men's ragged garments, broken shoes, and the rotting leather gloves of our archers now littered the roadside with increasing regularity. And, despite the guilt that still troubled me after our looting of Harfleur, I felt pleased that I had chosen to plunder a new pair of boots and tunic and not some mirror or cauldron or such as the Bowens still carried.

After a gruelling twelve miles or so our commanders called a rest. I slumped down at the roadside, unslung my pack and stretched out on the wet grass, glad of the opportunity to ease my aching legs.

"My feet are twice as big as they were when we left Harfleur," groaned Morgan as he took off his own ruined shoes and examined the weeping sores and blisters that covered his heels and soles. "I dearly wish I was back in Tregarth, taking my ease on our village green and drinking good beer. How far have we walked since that hellish place?"

"Eighty miles, I would say," said a voice behind us. "And now is certainly not the time to weaken or to complain, my lads!"

We all turned round to see the small, mud-spattered figure of Davy Gam staring down at us. Morgan looked as though he very much wished he'd held his tongue, fearing he might be flogged, or worse, as a result of his complaints. But Davy just grinned and said, "We'll soon be at the River Somme and the ford at Blanche-Taque, boys. It's the place where Edward III, our King's own great-grandfather, took his own army across the Somme on the way to his great victory at the Battle of Crécy. Once we're over that nothing should stand in our way. Calais is now only some forty or fifty miles to the north of us!"

"So, Davy!" said Wynn. "Does that mean that the rest of our journey will be nothing more than a summer's stroll through a meadow?"

"I wouldn't count on it, Wynn Vaughn," laughed Davy. "But all in all, boys, we aren't doing too badly. We should be safely at Calais in just a few days' march from here."

"But won't the French be planning some sort of major attack on us?" I said. "Surely they won't allow us to tramp through their land unhindered?"

"Our King has planned for that eventuality," said Davy. "Some days ago he sent his messengers to summon a force from Calais. It will act as a decoy to draw off any French army who may be seeking us."

Despite our feelings of exhaustion and hunger, Davy's words gave us much encouragement. As each step brought us nearer the ford over the Somme, my spirits rose. We even began to talk of homecomings and seeing our families again. But then, when we were within a few miles of the crossing place, we were suddenly halted. As we sat around, wondering what the delay might be, Wynn flagged down a mounted archer and asked him for news.

"Tell me, friend," said Wynn, "why are we stopped?"

The archer drew his horse to a halt, giving us a grave and downcast look as if considering whether or not to speak. Then he said, "The King's scouts have taken a prisoner. At first what this man said seemed so fantastical that the King did not believe him and said he would cut off his head if he discovered he was lying. But the man swore he was telling the truth."

"And what did he say?" asked Owen.

"That all of the French nobles have agreed to forget their squabbles," said the archer. "And that they are massing huge armies to cut us off before we can reach Calais."

"But surely," said Morgan, "if we can get across the ford we'll outmarch them and reach Calais in safety. Haven't we just some thirty miles to go?"

"That is true," said the archer. "But there is yet more bad news."

"And what is that?" I said, feeling my heart sink to my boots.

"The ford is guarded by 6,000 French soldiers," said the archer. "The same ones who were gathering across the river from us at Harfleur."

"Which must mean they have outmarched us!" groaned Wynn.

"Exactly!" said the man. "We aren't to cross the Somme after all."

"But what *are* we to do?" I cried.

"We can't go north across the river," he replied, "and it would be suicide to turn back for Harfleur. We have no choice but to follow the Somme's southern bank."

"But that means we'll be marching *away* from Calais and back into the heartlands of the French!" gasped Owen, looking as if he couldn't believe his ears.

"Yes," said the man. "It does."

And that is exactly what we did. We began to march *away* from Calais and, for the time being, away from all hope of escape from France.

All of those thoughts of heroism and triumph which had filled my head as our ship left England seemed to have vanished for ever. I felt as if I was trapped in some sort of never-ending hell-on-earth. Here we were, hundreds of miles from home, in a foreign land peopled almost entirely by those whose one desire was to kill us. We were starving, our army was outnumbered and we were shadowed by an enemy force that grew with each day that passed.

And of course, despite the efforts of surgeons, the bloody flux that had already taken so many of our number at Harfleur still troubled hundreds of our soldiers. As I have already told you, my own case was nowhere near as bad as some. However, like many of those afflicted, I still found it necessary to cut away the seat of my breeches, as the need to relieve myself came upon me so quickly and unexpectedly that I didn't have time to take them off in the normal manner. Never a day passed without at least half a dozen poor stinking, filth-smeared, flux-ridden wretches collapsing at the roadside, then dying in agony.

Occasionally, as I lay curled in a ball in some foul ditch, listening to the rain beating against my tattered cloak, or feeling the frost gripping my shivering limbs, I would slip into a fitful sleep and dream that I was back in Tregarth, warm and safe in my mother's cottage, sitting by the blazing log fire with Gryff asleep at my feet. But then I would wake, to find myself soaked to the skin or numb with cold. And now winter drew ever nearer. On one particularly cold and frosty morning I felt a sharp pain in the back of my head as I attempted to sit up. My hair had actually become frozen to the mud on which I lay! What a hopeless and desperate situation we were in, so different from our position all those long weeks ago in Harfleur. Now we had no choice but to push on, and to put our faith in God and our King.

Three days after turning south we reached the village of Boves. It was here that Wynn told us the King had promised the locals that their property would be untouched if our passage was unhindered.

"Take heed!" said Wynn. "The King is a man of his word. Don't be tempted by anything you happen to see lying about!"

"What!" joked Owen Bowen, attempting to bring some cheer to us all. "Not even tempted to *borrow* it?"

"No!" replied Wynn Vaughn, with a wry grin. "Not even to borrow it!"

Not everyone heeded the King's warning. The day after we left Boves we were told that a boy archer had been discovered with a precious box hidden under his tunic. He was believed to have stolen it from the church at Boves. When the King heard of the theft he was beside himself with rage and ordered his army to gather before him.

We all stood in silent lines as the archer was dragged in front of us. As he and his escort drew near I noticed that the thief had red hair. And then I received a terrible shock. I saw that the accused was none other than Tobias Simcock, the boy who had been so kind to me and helped me to the surgeon's tent when I had my attack of flux. I could hardly believe my eyes.

The wretched Tobias stood before us, his chin on his chest and his body racked by great sobs. The charges against him were then read out, the main one being that he had stolen from a church, and that, as we were on a mission of God, his crime was unforgivable. Now trembling from head to toe, Tobias was taken to an oak tree and seated upon a horse while a rope was slung from a branch above him.

I knew what would happen next and was desperate to turn my head away from the terrible sight which would surely follow. But we were all under strict orders to witness the fate of this archer. I had no choice but to keep my eyes fixed upon the weeping boy who had been so kind to me. Despite his pitiful pleas for mercy, a noose was placed around Tobias's neck. Then, as we all held our breath, a soldier slapped the horse hard on its flank and it galloped away. Instantly, Tobias was jerking in mid-air, then his skin went blue and I knew that he was dead.

All of us were made to file past Tobias's hanged body so that we would not forget the penalty that would await us if we too were tempted to steal from a French church.

My father had told me about executions he had witnessed during the troubles with the English but I had never seen anyone hanged before, least of all someone I had known personally. I felt quite sick and shaky as I looked up at the lifeless corpse which gently swung to and fro before my eyes. I can tell you, the sight came to haunt me in my dreams for many nights after and it is certainly something that I will never forget as long as I live.

In the early weeks of our campaign we had all fared well on our daily ration of two pounds of bread and half a pound of meat. But now our food supplies were as good as gone and I was ravenously hungry all of the time. In order to stave off the hunger pains which constantly gnawed at my empty stomach I began digging up and eating raw and muddy roots which I found in roadside fields. I also stuffed wild hedgerow fruits into my mouth as often as I could. It was hard to tell which were poisonous and which were not, and on one occasion I gulped down a bunch of fat, juicy and delicious-looking red berries, believing them to be edible, then, just moments later, found myself on my knees retching them up onto the mud. My wine and water were also all gone so I drank from streams and rivers and, if none were nearby, I simply sipped from muddy puddles.

Nature didn't desert us entirely. Since it was October, nuts were plentiful and we picked and ate them whenever the opportunity arose. We mostly ate hazelnuts and this caused some amusement amongst us, as in our part of the world they are said to make those who eat them wise and all-knowing.

"If I eat many more of these," said Owen, picking yet another handful of hazelnuts, "I will be the wisest boy in all Europe."

"That will be the day!" spluttered Morgan through a mouthful of nuts.

"In my village," said one archer, "they are fed to the cows and pigs. But they continue to be as stupid as the day they were born!"

"And so does my twin!" roared Morgan.

Our laughter at Morgan's joke was short-lived, though, and, desperate with hunger, we quickly returned to our frantic search of the hedgerows.

Nuts, roots, berries and pond water are no replacement for proper food and drink and we soon began to suffer the effects of not regularly eating wholesome meals. My bones poked through my skin, I had blinding headaches, I felt dizzy for much of the time and my teeth even became loose in my gums.

Our equipment and clothes were in just as sorry a state as we were. It rained almost every day and our armour and weapons quickly began to rust. Our hats and shoes also rotted in the constant dampness. Many men went bareheaded and barefoot, or made do with scraps of leather tied to the soles of their feet with rope.

I was also horribly filthy. I had been wearing the same clothes for more than eight weeks, fighting, marching through the mud and sleeping in roadside ditches and fields in them. As a result, my breeches and shirt were encrusted with a stinking filth which grew thicker each day. And, naturally, this filth attracted all manner of vermin. I was crawling with lice and fleas which crept and wriggled in every crack and crevice of my body, torturing my sore and itching flesh both day and night. As to my smell, I am sure it was so bad that the French could tell that I and my comrades-in-arms were coming from miles away, simply by sniffing the air. But, as we were all equally foul and fetid, it was hard to tell just how bad we all were.

I was continually exhausted. Not the tiredness you get after a hard day's field-work, but a deadly exhaustion that numbed my brain and body and made my every muscle feel as though it was made of lead. Sometimes, when I awoke in the mornings, I felt as if I'd slept for just minutes and it was only the terrifying thought of being left at the mercy of the French that made me crawl from under my rain-sodden cloak and drag myself to my feet to continue the trek. On one occasion I was so exhausted that I lost consciousness completely, falling asleep as I marched. I was woken by a searing pain across my forehead as I tripped in a pothole and slammed into the trunk of a roadside oak.

And so, in this sorry state, the King's army arrived at the place called Corbie. We couldn't have looked more different from the large force of splendidly turned-out French knights who took us all completely by surprise. They suddenly surged across the bridge, their warhorses snorting and whinnying and their lovely red, gold and blue banners streaming behind them as they thundered towards our leading archers. All of the knights were encased in gleaming armour which twinkled and flashed in the pale October sunlight and every one of them was armed with the finest of weaponry. As they bore down upon our brother archers, my companions and I gazed in awestruck terror at their two-handed lopping swords and wooden steel-tipped lances, each at least ten feet long. They carried battle-axes and lead truncheons; billhooks and razor-sharp disembowelling halberds, all of which they confidently thrust before them whilst letting out exuberant war cries. Our bowmen didn't stand a chance. Before they could fit shaft to bow, the huge hooves of the French knights' warhorses were pounding them into the earth with wild abandon.

Now, from our position on the right rear flank of our army, we saw our own mounted reinforcements quickly galloping up to join battle with the enemy. There followed a brief and bloody conflict during which our forces eventually gained the upper hand, both driving the knights back over the bridge and also taking half a dozen prisoners.

It sounds a strange thing to say, but this skirmish turned out to be a fortunate event, although it didn't seem so at the time. The prisoners told our interrogators that riding down our archers had been a deliberate tactic which the French knights intended to use on us again and again. This set the King to thinking about how best he could protect us from future attacks of this sort. And that is why, later that day, Davy Gam came to us and cried, "Boys! You are each to cut a stout, thick pole from the hedgerow, then sharpen it at each end. When we have cut these stakes we must carry them for the rest of our march."

The idea of carrying a wooden pole may not seem a particularly difficult task but, if you are exhausted and starving and marching twenty miles each day along broken roads in pouring rain, quite soon that pole no longer feels like a pole. In my case, it soon began to feel as heavy as iron and, for all I knew, I might as well have been carrying the whole tree from which I had cut it.

After we left Corbie, the King decided to change our route and head south across a loop in the River Somme. It was his hope that we might confuse, and possibly even evade, the French forces that we knew were constantly shadowing us on the opposite bank. That evening we arrived at a village called Nesle and, after the King had once more threatened to burn the villagers' crops and houses, they agreed we could spend the night in their barns. So, after we'd eaten the half-rotten potatoes and leeks I'd found hidden under some mouldering sackcloth, my friends and I crept into a leaky stable, climbed onto some piles of straw, and were soon fast asleep.

"Wake up, boys!" cried Wynn early the next morning, as he seized the still-snoring Owen and shook him into consciousness. "We are to cross the Somme!"

"But I thought the crossing places were guarded," I said, wearily dragging myself from my pile of straw.

"Or protected by barriers?" yawned Morgan.

"No, not all of them," said Wynn. "Last night the village leaders here talked to our King. They are sorely scared and wish to see us gone. Rather than seeing their homes burned they came to him in secret and told him of two fording places a few miles from here. He immediately sent his scouts to see if they spoke the truth."

"And did they?" I said.

"Yes!" said Wynn. "Not only are the fords crossable but they are unguarded. We move immediately. The pack animals and carts will go to the fording place called Bethencourt and the archers and men-at-arms will cross at the one they call Voyennes."

"But what if the French are waiting for us on the other side?" I asked.

"Our lords have thought of that," said Wynn. "They are sending an advance detachment of 200 archers to protect the army from a surprise attack, and we are to join them. So shake a leg and look lively. We leave in ten minutes."

We set off in the early morning darkness, lightly armed so that we could travel swiftly. At first we made good progress, encouraged by the thought of crossing the Somme and beginning the last leg of our march to Calais and home. As we neared the river, the ground became softer and I soon found myself tramping through a great sticky marsh. The mud sucked greedily at my feet with each step I took, slowing my progress and making my calves ache. A wooden causeway had been built across the swamp but it had many sections missing. Slinging our bows across our backs, we scrambled onto the remaining sections, then began jumping from one to the next, sometimes taking running leaps to vault the widest gaps. We took the utmost care lest we should lose our footing and plunge into the mud below, but Owen Bowen managed to do this very thing. With much flailing of arms and legs and a stream of oaths that I dare not repeat, he tumbled into the ooze with a soggy splash! Doing our best to stifle our laughter at the sight of him flopping about in the mire like a huge pig in a mud bath, we hauled Owen from the swamp before he could be sucked down even further.

By about eight o'clock we had reached the village of Voyennes and the wide River Somme which we would cross to form a bridgehead on the opposite bank and make the passage safe for our comrades. Cautiously, I stepped into the fast-flowing water, carefully feeling my way with my feet, fearing I might lose my footing and be swept away by some treacherous invisible current. Soon, the water was up to my waist, but fortunately the riverbed was firm so I was able to make slow but steady progress. As the current swirled about me I prayed constantly that a force of Frenchmen would not appear on the opposite bank, for if they did, we would all be at their mercy. Despite my fears we finally reached the far shore safely and a dozen or so archers scurried to the top of a grassy hillock to ensure that the enemy was not waiting in ambush. When they gave the all clear we climbed the bank, then settled ourselves on the high ground overlooking the river and marsh.

While I had been making my way through the marsh I had heard the sounds of axes crashing into wood as, somewhere behind us, the King's carpenters and labourers felled trees for timber to repair the broken causeway. As I waited on the hillside I began to spot teams of labourers hauling tree trunks towards the gaps. Soon, other groups of workers and foot soldiers appeared and, ignoring the terrified protests of the Voyennes peasants, they began attacking their cottages. They seized great bundles of thatching straw, tore down roof timbers, ripped doors from their frames, pulled gates from posts and even lifted away whole sections of walls. All of this material was then speedily carried or dragged onto the marsh where it was used to rebuild the wooden roadway. At about noon, the causeway seemed to be almost ready. It was then that I saw a figure on horseback moving slowly along it towards the river and recognized King Henry. He was inspecting the work of his labourers, ensuring that their hasty repairs were firm enough to support his army. After some moments he gave a signal and two of his nobles began to move along the roadway, followed by about 500 foot soldiers. They moved swiftly and steadily towards the riverbank where the King waited to supervise their passage across the Somme.

In the meantime, a little further along the riverbank at the Bethune crossing, two of the King's most trusted knights were performing a similar task, ensuring the safe and swift passage of the carts and pack animals.

I don't think more than 100 of the foot soldiers could have passed across the Voyennes ford when I heard a warning shout and turned, just in time to see a large band of mounted French knights galloping at great speed towards us. Unlike the incident at Corbie where we had been taken so badly unawares, we were completely prepared for just such an attack. As the knights reached the bottom of the hill, we let loose a fusillade of arrows that brought down at least six of them. Undaunted, the remainder continued their charge and, as I fitted a new arrow to my bowstring, 30 or 40 of them gained the midpoint of the slope that lay below us. I had not seen where my first arrows had fallen but I now saw one strike the horse of one of the leading French knights – a tall noble, dressed in yellow and black and carrying a red and gold shield. His horse immediately went down, catapulting him over its shoulders and causing the two horses directly behind to crash into it, also unseating their riders. Out of the corner of my eye I saw this scene repeat itself many times over as our arrows found their marks in French horses and riders alike. There followed chaotic scene, with riderless horses galloping this way and that. Unhorsed knights rushed up the slope towards us, swinging their war-axes above their heads and yelling furiously as they desperately tried to reach our lines. However, luck was with us because a large group of the soldiers who had just crossed the river came racing to our assistance and began attacking the knights from the rear. Seeing they were outnumbered, the remaining French knights galloped back in the direction from which they'd come, leaving the rest of our army to cross the river unhindered.

By the time night fell the whole of our army had successfully crossed the Somme. It looked as though we had just a few days' march to go before reaching Calais. I fell in to my bed, exhausted, but deeply satisfied by our efforts. I was sure that the sea was just a matter of days away and I soon began to dream of warm homecomings and reunions.

Two days later, at a crossroads near the town of Peronne, all thoughts of homecomings fled my mind like rats from a burning hayrick. For, as the rain lashed me in great, grey, drenching sheets and the wind whipped my soaked rags about my shivering body, we came upon a sight that made my heart sink and my legs turn to jelly. All across the ground before us, for as far as the eye could see, were the imprints of thousands of boots and many more thousands of horses' hooves. And cutting across them all were deep, water-filled ruts where wagons and gun carts had been dragged through the mud. It was quite plain to see that a vast army, many, many times greater than our own, had recently passed this way. We all stood as if struck dumb and stared in disbelief. After all the efforts of the past weeks, the hunger, the cold, the exhaustion, the sickness, the attacks by the French … this was almost too much to bear.

"It's them," said Owen in a whisper.

"And so many of them," mumbled Morgan.

"Thousands and thousands," said Wynn. "I've never seen anything like it."

Suddenly a voice somewhere in the ranks behind us set up a mournful wail. "O dear Lord God!" it cried. "Have mercy on us. In your infinite goodness turn away from us the power of the French. Allow us safe passage to our homes."

I turned to see that one of our priests had fallen to his knees in the mud and was holding his cross out in front of him as he beseeched God to spare us. Soon the others joined him in his prayers and one by one, all of the soldiers and archers who stood so miserably in the mud fell to their own knees and joined them in their pleas. And then, when we had made our prayers, we once more began our march, now certain that every step we took was bringing us nearer to our deaths.

24th – 25th October 1415

On 24th October, three days after we had seen all those thousands of foot and hoofprints at Peronne, we crossed the River Ternoise. Some time after this, still wet from our crossing, we came to a steep ridge that rose abruptly in front of us, preventing us from seeing our way ahead.

Our captains immediately signalled for us to halt. As we did, I noticed a single horseman break away from a group of nobles quite close to us and gallop to the top of the ridge. On reaching the summit he quickly brought his mount to a stop, obviously transfixed by what he saw. Like a stone statue silhouetted against the pale October sky, he remained perfectly still for some minutes. Then, quite suddenly, he turned his horse and galloped back down to the waiting nobles.

Wynn made his way up through the ranks, anxious to discover our situation. He returned some five minutes later, looking more grim-faced than ever.

"What news?" Owen Bowen asked nervously.

Wynn pointed to the hillside and said, "That ridge gives a perfect view of the valley beyond it. The mounted man you saw gallop to its summit was the Duke of York's scout. He is very shaken by what he has seen."

"Well, what *has* he seen?" I said.

Wynn took a deep breath, then said, "The village of Maisoncelles is just beyond the ridge, and a little further on, the villages of Tramecourt and Agincourt. But it is not the villages that concerned him. It is what he saw beyond them! He has informed the King that, at this very moment, thousands and thousands of our enemies are pouring into the valley. He says they are as numerous as locusts. At least six, possibly ten, times greater than us."

"So we're…" whispered Owen.

"Trapped," said Wynn. "There is no way we can avoid battle. The road to Calais is blocked by this great host of Frenchmen. We must fight them."

About half an hour later, just as the light was beginning to fade, our army made its way to the top of the ridge where we formed ourselves into a long line. What I saw when we looked down into that valley made my stomach churn, my heart pound and my legs feel as if they were made from bowstrings. There below us, about half a mile away, for almost as far as I could see in all directions, was a sea of grey steel. Moving before us was the most enormous host of men I had ever laid eyes on in my whole life. As their pennants fluttered in the breeze and their lances bobbed up and down, countless French knights on horseback were taking up their positions in the valley. And they were not all. This vast and never-ending forest of metal-clad cavalry men was accompanied by rank after rank of foot soldiers and crossbowmen who, in turn, were followed by all manner of war-machines and cannon. There seemed to be no end to their variety and number.

I don't know how long we stood there, but as darkness fell and the campfires of the enemy began to flicker below us, the King gave orders for us to leave the ridge and make our way down the slope. Then, on reaching the valley floor, we prepared to spend the night alongside the village of Maisoncelles, just half a mile or so from the place where the vast French army was gathered.

I think that night before the battle was the most miserable and terrifying of my whole life. It rained continually and, to make matters worse, Owen and many of the other archers had caught heavy colds, which caused them to sneeze and shiver constantly the whole night long.

I was also more tired than I'd felt in my whole life. Nevertheless, despite my exhaustion, I could not sleep. As I lay tossing and turning on the cold wet earth, the thought struck me that this was almost certainly going to be my last night in this world. Then, remembering all those thousands of coldly glinting lances, pikes, swords and maces we had seen just hours before, I began to wonder how I might die. Just as I was beginning to conjure up gruesome pictures of perhaps being spitted like a boar on a knight's lance and wondering how much pain I would suffer before I lost my reason or mercifully passed out, I felt a sharp prodding in my ribs and heard the voice of Owen Bowen.

"Jenkin, Jenkin!" he hissed. "Are you awake?"

"Yes," I replied, "I am. And if I hadn't been, I would be now. What is it you want?"

"I want to confess," he said, sniffing. "We are certainly going to die tomorrow and I wish to make my conscience clear with God."

"So why haven't you gone to the chaplains?" I muttered.

"If I had I would be waiting for ever," said Owen.

"Did you not see that long line of men waiting to confess?"

Owen was right. It seemed as though every man in the army had realized he was going to die and wanted to own up to his past sins in readiness for tomorrow.

"Tell me then," I said.

"Well," said Owen, "do you remember how in May your mother baked five large pies and left them out on your cottage windowsill to cool? And how those pies mysteriously disappeared?"

"Yes," I said, "I do."

"It was me who took them," said Owen, "and I ate them too."

"What, *all* of them?" I said.

"Yes," he said. "And for my sins I was terribly sick."

"Well, I forgive you then," I said.

Our two camps couldn't have been more different that night. As my companions and I lay subdued and fearful, occasionally whispering anxiously, a joyous racket arose from the enemy camp. Just across the fields from us, French knights, certain that they were on the eve of a great victory, were drinking and shouting and throwing dice to decide which of them should take which English noble prisoner. And

115

mingled with their raucous yells, we also heard the sound of drunken singing.

"They are in good spirits," I whispered.

"I'm not surprised," murmured Morgan Bowen. "They know we are weak and exhausted. They are sure of victory tomorrow."

As I dreamed yet another dream of all those thousands of footprints we'd seen at the crossroads near Peronne, I felt a hand tugging at my shoulder and opened one eye to see Morgan staring down at me in the early-morning darkness.

"Wake up, Jenkin," he said. "The others are up and about. It is time. We have to prepare ourselves. Today we face our greatest test of all."

Shivering with cold, I dragged myself from the damp and dismal hollow that had been our bed. Then, aching in every bone in my body and truly believing that I had just spent my last night on earth, I gathered my belongings. Just minutes later, our little group joined the columns of ragged and dispirited men trudging wearily out of Maisoncelles. It was still dark as we left the village but the rain had stopped, leaving the ground soft, with deep puddles covering the road that led to the valley where the French awaited us.

As the wagons and pack animals loaded with our provisions moved off towards the woods where they were to remain for the rest of that day, we finally reached the cornfield that separated us from the enemy. Davy Gam came and stood before us.

"Today, boys," he said, "we are to do battle with the French. As you have seen, their numbers are vast. But we must not be downhearted. During the night King Henry sent his scouts to survey the field. They discovered that the French are spread across a battlefront of just three quarters of a mile. On their left they are hemmed in by the woods of Tramecourt and on their right by the woods that surround the village and castle of Agincourt. And he thinks this will give us some advantage, as they will have little room for movement. Though it be a small mercy we must take heart from this news. And after that we must trust in God." With that, Davy and our captains began to draw us into our positions as directed by the King.

After some twenty minutes or so our army finally assumed its position, standing with its back to Maisoncelles in a long line of troops about four men deep. This line was split into three divisions. Our King commanded the central one, the Duke of York the right, and Lord Camoys the left. In between each stood groups of our archers in formations shaped like wedges. Then, on the far right and left flanks of this entire assembly of men stood two more large forces of archers. Each was placed at a slight angle to the main force, so that they might attack the French from the side when they made their advance. It was in the right-hand force of these flanking archers that I stood along with my three friends.

When we were in our places, the royal trumpeters raised their instruments in readiness to sound the call-to-arms. A few moments later, a figure mounted on a small grey horse appeared before us. It was King Henry. He was clad in a suit of splendidly shining armour, on top of which he wore a surcoat, the quarters being brilliantly embroidered with the arms of England and France, three leopards and the fleur-de-lys. A surge of pride seized my whole being as I looked upon my King, and a great lump came to my throat and my eyes grew moist.

Drawing his mount to a halt, the King calmly surveyed us. And then he spoke.

"Now is the time," he cried, "for all England prays for us. Let us be of good cheer and go to our journey!" And then, after giving us these words of encouragement, he rode away. He was followed by pages leading his other mounts, amongst which was a warhorse, as beautiful and as snowy-white as the swans which had flown over our fleet at Spithead all those weeks before.

Priests came and stood before us and prayed for our success. As they made their pleas to God to give us victory and to bring us safely through the day, I looked past them towards our enemy, who stood about half a mile away. At that distance it was hard to tell much about the French. All I can say is, at that moment, they appeared to me as nothing more than a vast and invincible wall of grey metal. We had no way of telling how many we finally faced that day, some say 40,000, others say 50,000, or even 60,000. But I can honestly tell you that, as I gazed across at that enemy host, I was seized by such dread that my innards turned to liquid and I wished myself anywhere else in the world but on this muddy cornfield in France.

As the priests continued their chanting, I looked to my fellow archers. What a pathetic sight they were, with their sunken eyes, gaunt faces, runny noses, tattered clothes and half-starved bodies, as they stood there, sniffing and sneezing in the chill morning air. And I wondered how such an exhausted, hungry and dispirited group of men and boys could possibly withstand an onslaught from such an army as the one that stood before us.

"Yes," I thought, "we really are King Henry's scarecrow army."

We stood in line and waited for the battle to commence. And we waited. And we waited. The French did not move and nor did we. We simply watched each other. First one hour passed. Then another. And then a third. And still we waited.

"Maybe they're waiting for us to surrender," muttered Owen Bowen, as we restlessly shuffled our feet in the wet earth and began our fourth hour of waiting.

"If they are, they'll be sorely disappointed." I said. "See, Owen! Our King has returned, and now he is prepared for battle."

King Henry had ridden to the front of our ranks, now mounted on his white warhorse. Once more he spoke to us, telling us how we had come to France to claim his rightful inheritance and how we must strive to return to England with glory and honour. And then he directed his words to us, his archers.

"Archers!" he cried. "My spies have been about their business during the night. They have discovered that if the French take any of you alive they will cut three fingers from your right hand so that you may never draw a bowstring again."

As the King spoke these words an angry murmur passed through our lines and I turned to Wynn and whispered, "Can this be true? Will they really do this thing?"

"Of course they will," said Wynn. "But take heart, Jenkin. Their threat is a tribute to us. Their plan to deprive us of our bow fingers means that they truly fear our reputation. It is now our duty to show them that they are right to do so."

As I listened to Wynn's and the King's words the hairs on the back of my neck stood on end. I knew that something more important than anything I had known in my whole life was about to take place. I silently vowed to be courageous in the coming battle in the hope that I would prove myself true to both my father and the great king who had brought me to France.

As the day edged towards noon, and just when I was beginning to feel that I would remain rooted to that field for all eternity, there was a sudden flurry of activity amongst the King and his nobles. After some minutes' conversation, Sir Thomas Erpingham moved towards us and began organizing us into tighter formations. Finally, something was about to happen. Having satisfied himself that we were properly prepared, Sir Thomas hurled his baton into the air and cried, "Now, strike!" and we answered him with a huge shout, for we knew that the moment of truth was almost upon us.

Next, Sir Thomas joined the King, who gave the command we'd been awaiting.

"Banners ... advance!" he cried. "In the name of Jesus, Mary and St George!"

At that instant all of the soldiers in that tired and tattered army of King Henry's dropped to one knee and we all did likewise. Then, after making the sign of the cross, we each took a piece of earth in our mouth and offered a silent prayer to God. As our trumpets began to sound and our comrades gave shouts of "St George! St George!", we all rose to our feet and slowly began to advance towards the enemy.

All the time I kept my eyes on the mass of Frenchmen who stood before us. Occasionally, a partridge or hare would break cover quite close to me, making me start in surprise, so great was my tension and apprehension.

"This is it then, Jenkin," said Owen, as he walked in line at my side. "Afraid?"

"Not really," I lied. "I think I feel more excitement than fear." But as I said these words, a great claw of naked fear gripped me and my heart thumped so wildly that I thought it would burst through my jerkin.

We were already almost halfway across the cornfield and it was possible to distinguish all the different sorts of fighting-men that made up the French army. At the front of their ranks stood unmounted knights, all of them encased in suits of hard steel and grasping the war-axes and mallets which they would soon be using to reduce our flesh to chopped meat. Behind them stood archers and crossbowmen, while on their flanks were the cannon and their gunners. But, fearsome as these sights were, it was the knights on horseback that held my gaze and made my blood run cold. Countless hundreds of them stood on either flank of the unmounted men, and behind the foot soldiers were many thousands more. All of them sat astride huge warhorses, each one draped in brilliantly coloured silks. These mounts were entirely without armour, apart from an occasional steel helmet.

We had advanced to within almost 400 yards of the enemy and, despite the exhaustion of the previous days, I suddenly felt as alive and alert as though I had rested for months. My heart raced, the blood fizzed and popped in my ears, my every nerve and muscle was as keyed and taut as a drawn bowstring. I was ready for anything.

Suddenly the urgent shout of Sir Thomas Erpingham rang out across the cornfield. It was followed by the sound of trumpets. That was all we needed. Battle had begun. Like one many-legged beast of war, we rushed forward, and then, just as we'd been instructed by Davy Gam, we raised our stakes high into the air and thrust them into the soft earth, tilting their vicious points towards the waiting Frenchmen.

Having ensured our poles were planted firmly, we fell back six or seven paces, halted again and turned to face the French. Next, at the shout of "Notch!" from our commanders, we took our arrows from our belts and slid them onto our bowstrings. After that came the command "Stretch!" and, just as we'd done so many times in our practice at the village butts, we pulled back our strings until we could feel those goose feathers touching our cheeks, and we carefully took aim. Then, as we waited for the third and final command of "Loose!" … we held our fire.

With my eyes narrowed and my teeth gritted, I heard fierce battle cries rise up from the massed ranks of Frenchmen and I saw a rippling movement pass along their front line, as though it were a silver serpent flexing its coils in readiness to strike. Then I saw them raise their swords and lances and step forward, while their huge scarlet banner flapped its angry challenge. At the same time, the mounted French knights spurred their warhorses into action and began to lumber towards us. At last it was happening. The enemy was attacking.

The unmounted knights were slow and cumbersome in their advance, weighed down by their heavy armour and hampered by the thick clinging mud of the field. But it was not so with their mounted companions. The knights had soon urged their horses into a headlong gallop and now, as they bore down on us at an absolutely terrifying pace, my ears filled with the sound of hundreds of hooves pounding soft earth while the very cornfield itself seemed to tremble in fear.

A great and seemingly indestructible wall of unyielding armour, sinew and razor-sharp steel was thundering relentlessly towards us. Despite my new-found courage, beads of sweat broke out on my forehead and my mouth became as dry as a hearthstone. What chance did we stand against such an onslaught? We were nothing more than a band of half-starved men and boys, bedraggled and filthy tramps, protected only by the rags we stood up in and the bows we gripped so fiercely. But did we turn and run from this monster? No, we didn't, for we knew so much depended on us. Ignoring my racing heart and my trembling knees, I simply planted my feet even more firmly in the soft mud of that cornfield and once more remembered my father's words. Then, facing this terror to end all terrors, I continued to hold my fire.

Soon the charging knights were so close to us that it was possible to see the faces of those that had raised their visors. But, even though they had exposed themselves so carelessly, still I held my fire, all the time keeping one eye on the baton which Sir Thomas Erpingham held high above his head and the other on the charging enemy.

And then it happened. Our trumpets blared their unmistakable message and Sir Thomas hurled his baton high into the air. It felt as though I had been waiting for this moment since that day, eight years earlier, when my father had handed me my first bow. As though we were one man, 5,000 of us released our bowstrings and the air was instantly filled with a great and terrifying whooshing sound. It was like a cruel winter's wind rushing through a mountain pass, or 5,000 snakes hissing their deadly warning, but many, many times louder. The pale autumn sun was immediately blotted out, as if by a vast flock of winged demons, and a huge, dark and ominous shadow fell across the oncoming Frenchmen.

To the constant cries of "Notch! Stretch! Loose!", we fitted fresh arrows, pulled back our strings and fired again. And then again. And again. And we did not stop firing. Thousands and thousands of our arrows soared skywards, then fell with deadly effect onto the oncoming enemy. As the steel-tipped shafts descended among them, the charging knights vainly attempted to avoid this lethal blizzard of death. Some leaned forward, as if to protect themselves from a sudden shower of rain, others raised their shields above their heads, while some zig-zagged this way and that, madly trying to avoid the deathly deluge. But, despite all of their efforts, our arrows found their marks. Soon, screaming foot soldiers were falling to their knees, arrows projecting from their necks, shoulders, heads and backs. Others continued to run on, regardless of the shafts that protruded from them, before finally collapsing into the mud.

It was the charging cavalry who bore the cruellest brunt of our barrage. As our arrows penetrated their armour, knights slipped from their mounts, crying out in agony. Horses went down too, trapping their riders beneath them. They would attempt to regain their feet, but crash to the ground again as yet more of our arrows thudded into their tortured flesh. Suddenly, all of the ground before us was littered with unhorsed knights, fallen mounts and running men, caught up in a frenzy of pain and panic. Some of them had been spiked by so many dozens of our arrows that they looked like human hedgehogs as they rushed this way and that, desperately seeking a way out of this nightmare that had come upon them so unexpectedly.

But, even though the King's army did not cease its furious onslaught for one moment, still the French came on. So vast were their forces that wave after wave of foot soldiers now began to surge towards us. At the same time, hundreds of mounted knights poured out from the trees behind them, urging their horses forwards with kicks and shouts as they swerved round their running foot soldiers, leaped over dead and wounded comrades, or simply trampled them into the mud.

Soon, the charging horsemen filled the whole of the field before us, just 40 yards or so from our fence of sharpened stakes. But, to my astonishment, they raced towards them as if they did *not* exist, seemingly unaware of the threat they presented to both man and mount. And then the truth struck me. To them they did not exist! From the far side of the field the stakes must have been unnoticeable, blending perfectly with the field's brown earth. But now, as they covered those final few yards, I saw the knights furiously trying to rein back their galloping mounts. At last, it seemed as though they had spied the peril that rose so terrifyingly from the ground before them. But their desperate efforts came too late. Caught up in the momentum of their forward rush and forced onwards by the sheer weight and push of animals behind them, the leading horses could do nothing other than crash headlong into our fence of spikes.

If you are a lover of horses, I would ask you to forgo reading of what happened next, for what befell those animals hardly bears telling. Soon the ground in front

129

of us appeared to be filled with a mass of screaming horses, some running in circles, others thrashing about wildly in an effort to free themselves from the stakes on to which they'd crashed. Many of those behind them, seeing what had befallen the poor beasts leading the charge, turned and began to race back towards their own lines, smashing into unhorsed knights and the mass of charging foot soldiers as they went. And all the time we continued to fire volley after volley of arrows into the struggling throng, making living pincushions of men and horses alike.

Some of the fallen knights attempted to rise from the ground, but the sheer weight of their armour prevented many of them from doing so and they collapsed back into the mud, only to be crushed under more oncoming cavalry or pounded into the ground by panic-stricken retreating horses. Those that did manage to struggle to their feet began to run towards us, waving their swords and axes, but such was the swirling chaos of the crush around them that their progress was slow.

By now, this throng of Frenchmen, both wounded and unwounded, was just yards from our nearest line of bowmen and suddenly these archers' bows were of little use to them. Throwing them to the ground, they gave a great shout. Then, rushing at the fallen and unhorsed men-at-arms, they took their swords and daggers and hammers from their belts and began slashing and stabbing and clubbing at them with wild abandon. As they rained down blow after blow, the fallen knights rolled this way and that, attempting to avoid their fury, but, held down by their armour, they stood little chance of avoiding the welter of blows that were soon smashing bones and splitting flesh.

The archers were not the only ones to have plunged into this mighty battle. Some yards to the left of me, I spotted a crowd of men setting about a pair of French knights and I realized that the wild Irishmen I had seen on the quayside in England had joined in the slaughter. They were furiously leaping upon the stricken knights, uttering wild and savage war cries as they did.

Firing a final arrow at a retreating French knight, I threw down my own bow and prepared to hurl myself into this mighty fracas. But then I felt someone grasp my arm and turned to see that it was Owen Bowen.

"Leave the bloodletting to the others, Jenkin!" he yelled. "Now is our chance to make our fortunes. See, the hostage-taking has begun! There are rich ransoms to be had. We cannot let this chance go begging!"

I looked to where he had pointed and saw that not all of the French knights had suffered such terrible fates as those who were being slaughtered. Many, realizing that they were completely at our mercy, had already taken off their gauntlets and were offering them up as a sign of their surrender. Some of our archers and knights had begun driving groups of these beaten and terrified nobles away from the battlefield, prodding at them and poking them as they shepherded them towards a cluster of wooden shacks at the edge of the field.

"Come on, what are we waiting for?" yelled Owen, and we quickly joined his brother Morgan, who was already driving a pair of dazed-looking French knights before him. A few minutes later we had secured our captives in a shed and, leaving the twins to guard the prisoners, I dashed back onto the field of combat, hoping that I might take at least one more hostage before all of the enemy were slain. Once more I heard the sound of trumpets and saw Sir Thomas Erpingham rushing amongst our archers, ordering them to their bows again. For he had seen what they had not. Whilst the mindless and frenzied attack on the fallen knights had been taking place, the vast French forces who still waited on the far side of the field had launched a massive new assault. A line of unmounted French knights, five or six deep and half a mile wide, was rapidly bearing down upon us. Quickly responding to Sir Thomas's urgings, I rushed back to my position, seized my bow, fitted an arrow to the string and again let loose my arrow.

The skies darkened again as our shafts rained down upon the enemy. As our razor-edged arrowheads found their mark, knights began to topple forwards, often bringing down their running comrades, so closely packed was this new assault. But so great were their numbers that still they came on, regardless of the showers of arrows flying towards them. It soon began to seem to me that for every Frenchman felled, six or seven more would take his place and that their ranks were without limits. They surged ever forwards, intent on reaching our King and his nobles, who awaited them at the centre of our army's ranks.

When they were almost upon them I heard our King utter a blood-chilling war cry as he and his men-at-arms rushed to meet the charging Frenchmen. With a deafening roar, the two armies cannoned into each other like gigantic iron-clad bulls, and there was an almighty crash as steel suit smashed into steel suit, helmet clashed with helmet, and blade bit into blade.

Then, to my alarm, I saw King Henry and his men-at-arms stagger backwards, overwhelmed by the sheer weight and numbers of the French attack. It now seemed to me as though our monarch and his nobles might be killed or captured, in spite of the constant barrage of arrows we continued to unleash upon their attackers.

As the King and his men fell back even further, the French pressed forward, eager to claim their prize. However, as more and more of them attempted to squeeze into the ever-narrowing gap between the trees that stood on either side of them, they became more and more hemmed in. Soon, in their desperation to reach our leader, they became so closely wedged that they found it difficult, even impossible, to lift their weapons above waist-height. And, as the great mass of their comrades continued to push them from behind, their situation grew worse. Seeing their advantage, the King and his men once more hurled themselves at the enemy. Wielding their axes and swords like madmen they began to attack the tightly packed wedge of French knights who struggled so helplessly before them.

All at once, I saw the whole struggling mass of French knights begin to sway, almost as if they were welded together. As one after another of them crashed to the ground, they would take five, maybe six comrades with them. The French knights were toppling like skittles and soon a heap of them lay sprawled in the mire, their legs and arms waving uselessly like the claws of overturned crabs. Soon their bodies were piled three, four … even five high.

Once again all of our army's archers threw down their bows and rushed at the French, setting about them with their axes and mallets. Just as before, they were joined by the screaming, savage Irishmen and the spear-wielding Flemings. In no time at all, the mud beneath their feet became slippery with the blood of the enemy, making it difficult for them to keep their footing – it was even worse for the steel-clad knights.

I hurled myself into this melee and, as men fought and struggled and cursed all around me, I was suddenly confronted by two French knights who had not only managed to rise from the blood-drenched mud, but also still held their weapons. They began to swing and jab at me and, as I backed away from them, dancing this way and that to avoid their blows, I found myself forced up against a great pile of bodies. All at once it looked like I might suffer the fate that had befallen so many of our enemies and die in agony on this hellish field. But then I heard a frenzied yell and saw a group of the wild Irishmen come racing to my rescue. As one of the French knights lunged at me with the wide, flat blade of his sword, an Irish warrior leaped onto his back and struck him a mighty blow with his lead mallet. A moment later his comrades were pounding the man to a lifeless bloody pulp.

Then, with a blood-curdling war cry, the Irishmen rushed off in pursuit of the knight's companion, who was now doing what hundreds of other French nobles were doing. He was fleeing the battle, scrambling wildly over piles of corpses and frantically throwing off his armour as he went.

But the frenzy of battle was at last subsiding and many of my comrades were now busily taking jewellery and weapons from the slain and wounded. Others were rounding up French knights who were surrendering in their hundreds. All at once it hit me that the thing that so many of us had not dared believe possible could be happening – we might have defeated our foes. I was suddenly so overwhelmed with such powerful feelings of relief that I thought I might break down and weep on the spot. As I watched a huge crowd of French prisoners being shepherded into a large clearing near the woods, I became aware of a friendly voice quite close to me and turned to see Wynn Vaughn standing at my side.

"Well, Jenkin Lloyd," he panted, wiping his blood-drenched dagger upon his breeches, "it looks like we may have seized the day. Although I am reluctant to say so just yet, as a large force of Frenchmen are still waiting in the trees to the north of us."

"I can hardly believe this victory," I said. "I truly expected to die here today."

"As did the rest of us," growled Wynn.

"What's going to happen to those French nobles?" I asked, pointing to the ever-growing throng of prisoners. "Are they all to be ransomed?"

"Only the very highest ranks will be ransomed," Wynn said grimly. "The King has ordered the others killed. He fears that there are so many prisoners that they will soon turn on us. If the French forces in the woods were to attack at the same time, we could be overwhelmed. But as for ransoms, many of our men are angry that they will not get to collect them. Some are even saying they will refuse to carry out the King's orders."

But the King's orders were carried out. As Wynn and I watched, King Henry rode amongst our forces and selected 200 archers to carry out the slaughter of the French knights. I am glad to say that we were not amongst their number. After warning these bowmen that any who refused his orders would be hanged on the spot, the King commanded them to begin their terrible task. Twenty minutes later, many more thousands of Frenchmen lay dead on the blood-soaked ground before us. And while this bloody slaughter was taking place, the knights whom we'd imprisoned in the huts earlier in the battle were also dispatched, but this took place without blood-letting. The huts were torched and the French knights burned alive inside them.

And so it was that Wynn and I came to be standing on that gore-drenched killing-field, dazed and exhausted as we surveyed the terrible carnage. I was still scarcely able to believe that our tiny army had defeated this vast multitude of Frenchmen.

It was early afternoon and we had been fighting for three whole hours. Carrion crows flapped and cawed above us and the smoke from the burning huts drifted through the bare trees. Our exhausted soldiers at last saw that victory really was theirs and a few simply collapsed at the side of the field, drained by all they'd seen and done. As Wynn went off in search of the Bowens, I joined those who sat at the field's edge, too exhausted from the battle and too shocked by the slaughter of the prisoners to involve myself immediately in the pillaging.

Before me I saw Welshmen, Englishmen and Irishmen scurrying from corpse to corpse, ripping off armour and clothes and frantically searching for valuables. Even though there was far more than they could possibly carry they squabbled over booty. Some, having difficulty removing the jewellery of the nobles, had even begun to hack off their fingers and hands, so desperate were they for the spoils of war. But, shocking though all this may seem, in many ways I could not blame them. Most of us had owned nothing all our lives, save the clothes we stood up in. Almost all of us came from hovels and cottages where we barely managed to get by. Even our lives weren't our own, but were pledged to the lords of our manors, for whom we toiled each day and of whom we lived in fear. And now, lying before us were thousands of the richest men in France, all clad in the finest armour, jewellery and clothes that money could pay for. And it was all there for the taking. This is what most of my comrades had come for. The reason they'd braved death and disease at Harfleur, endured starvation, attack and exhaustion on the roads of France and risked the terrors of battle.

And we also knew that, had the victory gone to the French, they would have shown us no mercy and slaughtered us all without hesitation. The life of a common soldier was not worth even one halfpenny of ransom money.

A band of the wild Irishmen strutted past me, dressed in the blood-drenched silks and mud-spattered armour of French nobles, delightedly waving the daggers that they'd taken from enemy corpses. With horror, I saw that one of them clutched the severed head of a French noble, gripping its long, bloodied hair and gleefully swinging it round his own head as he capered amongst the dead and dying. They were followed by a group of archers. All of them were quite drunk and singing and shouting victoriously as they swigged from looted wine flasks and staggered under the enormous weight of their plunder. One giant of a fellow had taken a blood-stained saddle from a French warhorse and, having put it on his back, was making neighing noises and cantering around the corpses that littered the cornfield, much to the amusement of his drunken friends. A little further across the field I noticed a group of mounted archers galloping after a herd of riderless French warhorses which were running wildly through the heaps of corpses, as if desperately searching for their butchered owners. Some ten minutes later the archers had managed to catch at least ten of these beasts and immediately began loading them with plundered armour and weaponry.

Feeling slightly better, I decided to set off in search of my comrades and join them in helping myself to the spoils of war. Rising unsteadily from the grass, I began to make my way along the edge of the cornfield. Having decided that my best plan would be to walk back towards Maisoncelles, I cut across the corner of the woods, then followed the line of a shallow ditch that seemed to head south.

Without warning, a French knight stepped from behind the trunk of a large oak tree. Before I could gather my wits, he swung at me with his war-hammer and struck me a savage blow on my right arm. A feeling of gut-wrenching pain ran from my shoulder to my hand and I looked down to see that my arm dangled uselessly at my side. As I did, the knight struck a blow to my face which made my brains rattle and my mouth fill with blood. Shocked by the fury and unexpectedness of this attack, I staggered away from my assailant. It was then that I saw he was wounded. Protruding from his chest were two broken arrow shafts and below them a great red stain was rapidly spreading across his breastplate, while blood dripped steadily onto the grass at his feet. Seeing his wounds gave me courage and I quickly feigned a stagger, hoping to draw him towards me. My feint worked and he swung at me with his mace, and this time I nimbly dodged the fearsome weapon. At that moment, the knight suddenly gave a groan and slumped against me. Then I felt him shudder, go limp, and sigh, and we both fell into the ditch. I think I must have passed out with the pain of my wounds at that point.

When I came to I found that I was lying in at least six inches of muddy water with the knight slumped across the lower half of my body. He was completely still and his blood was turning the ditchwater a deep crimson. I managed to pull myself into a semi-sitting position so that I was able to see beyond the banks of the ditch, but on trying to move further, to my horror I discovered that I was firmly wedged beneath him, my thighs being pinned down by his massive weight.

The ditch was not far from the field and through the trees I could still see our soldiers running back and forth between the bodies. I tried crying out for help, but my words came out as feeble moans that went unheeded by the looters. I attempted to move again but, try as I might, I could do no more than wriggle weakly under the dead man's huge weight.

I couldn't believe it! I was in the same position as those Frenchmen who lay dead and dying on the field, crushed and trapped by a knight in armour. "To have survived all that I have endured in the past weeks," I thought, "only to end up dying in this miserable ditch."

My only hope now was that a comrade would stumble upon me and rescue me. In the meantime I decided to lie still and rest in the hope that my energy would return and eventually give me sufficient strength to cry out or try to escape once more. Then I passed out again.

When I awoke it was late afternoon and the rain had begun again. My body ached all over as if I had been trampled on by a herd of cattle and my swollen right arm felt as big as a tree trunk. As I raised my head and peered through the trees I saw that the battlefield was empty of our troops, although in the distance I could still make out small groups of soldiers lurching off in the direction of Maisoncelles. They were almost invisible under their great piles of plunder. As they finally disappeared from sight I began to notice shadowy figures furtively emerging from the woods at the opposite edge of the battlefield. Casting nervous glances this way and that, they would dash towards a corpse, grab what they could, then rush back to the cover of the trees.

With the ever-increasing gloom, these marauders grew in number and became bolder in their forays until large groups were wandering around the battlefield. From their ragged clothes and hangdog manner, it occurred to me that these were French peasants from the surrounding villages, eager to share in the spoils of our victory. And where these peasants weren't busily thieving, scavengers of the feathered sort were also hard at work. Flocks of huge black crows, rooks and jackdaws were descending on the field in their hundreds and hopping from corpse to corpse.

As the peasants melted into the shadows, it seemed that almost every corpse on that battlefield had been stripped completely and lay naked in the gloom. They were lit by the eerie glow from the huts where the hostages had been burned and from a fire that blazed somewhere near Maisoncelles. My blood ran cold as I saw yet another scavenger lope silently onto the battlefield. Great grey wolves were slinking out of the distant trees and heading for the corpses. They sniffed curiously at the ghostly white bodies, almost as if they could not believe their good fortune.

Fearing that sooner or later one of these beasts would discover me and make a meal of my own, still-living flesh, I made one last almighty effort to pull myself from the ditch. Doing my best to make as little noise as possible and ignoring the pain that surged so savagely through my arm and aching jaw, I grasped a tussock of coarse grass with my uninjured left arm, and began to pull myself up. I think if I had not spent all those hours of practice at our village butts I would not have been able to rise one single inch, but, as I have told you, the pulling arm and shoulder of an archer is a remarkable thing. After a few minutes I was more than halfway out, but then, to my frustration, all of my energy seemed to ebb from my body once more and I could go no further.

It was at this point that I saw a grey shape slowly padding towards me. By the light from the distant fires I could plainly see the long pink tongue that lolled from its open jaws and the devilish red eyes which were now firmly fixed upon me. Despite my efforts to avoid attracting their attention, one of the wolves had found me, and I was completely at its mercy.

"So this is it," I thought. "This is my end. I am to be eaten alive."

The wolf was so close to me that I could hear its rapid panting and smell the foul, meaty odour of its breath. My heart knocked wildly against my ribs. In a moment I would surely feel its yellow fangs sink into my trembling flesh. But then I heard a familiar swishing sound and saw an arrow firmly embed itself in the creature's flank, then another thud into its throat. Giving a howl of anguish that might have woken all the dead of the battlefield, the wounded beast sank to the earth and, as a great shudder passed down the length of its body, it too breathed its last.

"Jenkin!" said a voice behind me. "You're alive!" I looked round and saw Wynn and the Bowens emerging from the shadows, clutching their bows.

"Jenkin!" gasped Owen. "We've been searching for you for hours."

"We thought you were dead," said Morgan, "or taken by the French."

"I was attacked by this French knight," I gasped as my friends bent to grasp the arms and legs of the armour-clad corpse that had pinned me down for so long. "We fell into this ditch. I think my arm may be broken. Some of my teeth too."

"But you're alive, Jenkin!" exclaimed Wynn. "That is what counts."

As it turned out, my arm wasn't broken but, like so many other parts of my body, it was caked in clotted blood and covered in purple bruises. These injuries were giving me so much pain that my comrades had to support me as I staggered across the battlefield and finally along the muddy lane that led to our camp. And it was as Wynn and the twins helped me into the village that I saw the source of the great blaze that had lit up the corpses on the battlefield so eerily. Just outside Maisoncelles, at the spot where a barn had stood earlier that day, there was now a huge heap of smouldering timbers and white ash. Smoke still billowed from it and showers of sparks and flames occasionally erupted, lighting up the surrounding fields. As we neared it, I once more smelled the terrible stench of burned human flesh.

"Did the French do that?" I asked, as we passed the glowing pile.

"No," said Morgan. "The barn was set on fire on the orders of the King. After the battle and the looting that followed he decreed that no man should take away more plunder or armour than he could carry or wear himself. So all the extra horseloads of booty that were brought up from the field were carried into the barn."

"The King had all of our own slain fighting-men taken in there too," said Owen. "There were about a hundred of them, or so we were told by the archers who carried their bodies from the battlefield. The barn was then set ablaze and their corpses burned along with the plunder."

"So few dead!" I gasped, remembering the thousands of French bodies lying in the cornfield. "How can that be?"

"Jenkin," said Owen, "a remarkable thing has happened here today. Through the grace of God and our own courage, tenacity and skill, King Henry's little ragtag army has defeated a mighty force of the most powerful and best-equipped fighting-men in all of France. The King's officials have reported that at least seven, possibly eight thousand French knights now lie dead in the cornfield."

"And what of our own nobles?" I asked.

"A handful perished in the battle," said Wynn. "Amongst their number was the King's cousin, the Duke of York. His body was found unwounded beneath a pile of armoured French corpses. The visor of his helmet was pressed into the mud and, being unable to open it, he quickly suffocated. But he hasn't been burned with the common soldiers. The King has ordered his body to be put into a vat and boiled until the flesh falls from his bones. Then his skeleton is to be taken back to England for burial."

That night, as we sat around our campfire, everyone had countless tales to tell of all that had happened during the extraordinary three hours when we had fought the French. When I had finished telling my own story of the encounter with the French knight, Wynn told us how he had witnessed the heroism of our King and his bodyguard of Welsh archers led by Davy Gam. They had rescued the Duke of Gloucester from a group of French nobles and, as the Duke lay wounded, King Henry had stood astride him, protecting him from his attackers. Eventually the French were driven off but during the fight Davy had been mortally wounded. As he lay bleeding in the mud, King Henry had stepped up to him and touched him on each shoulder with his sword, saying, "Davy Gam, I create thee a knight." Not long after this, our brave Davy had died in the arms of his pages.

And then, our tales finally told and our energy gone, we wished each other goodnight and sank back onto our beds of straw. As I drifted off to sleep, my wounded bow arm twitched and jerked constantly, as if I were still in the midst of the great battle. And in my mind's eye I saw flocks of our arrows falling amongst the stricken Frenchmen over and over again.

The following day our army left Maisoncelles and made its way north along the road that led across the cornfield. All around us lay thousands of French corpses. In the morning light it was possible to see their horrible wounds which, in many cases, had been made worse by the scavenging wolves and crows. Occasionally we would see a wounded Frenchman rise up and attempt to flee but he would soon be captured. If he were a noble he would be put along with the prisoners who had survived the slaughter, but common soldiers would simply be killed, having no ransom value at all.

Every one of us was weighed down with plunder, as were all of our army's horses and all those mounts taken from the French. Exhaustion and hunger made for slow progress and we covered no more than a few miles each day. When we finally reached Calais on 29th October many of us were so desperately hungry that we were forced to sell much of our plunder to the people there so that we could buy food. I had to sell the silver dagger and the jewellery that my friends had taken from the body of the French knight who had trapped me. Owen Bowen reluctantly handed his cherished mirror to a baker in exchange for some loaves of bread while Morgan traded his prized pans for money to buy ale and beef. But, despite being tired and hungry, we had just one more leg of our trip to complete. All we had to do was to wait for the ships to come from England so that we could finally make our sea crossing home.

To our disappointment, this wait turned out to be a lengthy one, and we were stuck in dreary Calais for many dismal weeks as winter storms prevented our ships from reaching us speedily. However, some time in the middle of November our fleet finally arrived and the King gave orders for our return.

If I had thought the sea we had crossed back in sunny August had been a turbulent one, it was a millpond compared with that which we encountered on our return journey. Hardly had we left port when a storm blew up and gales began to tear at the sails and rigging of our boats. Giant waves battered at the woodwork and both men and horses were thrown about the decks. During this great tempest two of our fleet sank with all on board, but our own ship, along with most of the fleet and that of our King, eventually made it safely to Dover.

So, as an early winter blizzard whipped round my ears, we finally set foot on English soil again. Our King was greeted by the local nobles who, being so utterly overjoyed at the news of our victory, waded out through the freezing waves so that they might triumphantly carry him ashore from his longboat.

Having unloaded our horses and weapons and what little remained of our supplies and the plunder, we began the march to London across the chalk downlands of the English county called Kent. During this march, a few of our fellow archers slipped away to their homes but, having a mind to see the City of London, the Bowen twins, Wynn and I remained with the King's army.

On 23rd November, we came to the wide and grassy plain called Blackheath, which stands above the River Thames, just a few miles from the City of London. It was here that I spotted a distant and ever-growing patch of red which looked like a rapidly spreading stain of blood. After some minutes I realized that this was no bloodstain but a vast crowd of many thousands of people, all of whom were wearing scarlet robes. They were rapidly making their way towards us and shortly we began to hear excited cheering and shouting. The overjoyed citizens of London had come out to welcome us, their returning and victorious army! Soon they all stood before us and their leader, the Lord Mayor of London himself, approached our King and offered him his congratulations on his great victory. The King accepted with dignity while the crowds all cheered us to the skies.

As one great joyful procession, we began to walk the final miles to London. It soon seemed that we could not pass through a hamlet or cluster of dwellings without more and more folk rushing from their houses, cottages and inns and joining us in our victorious cavalcade.

In a short while we entered the village they call Southwark and it was here that, above all the noise of the jubilant crowds who lined our route, I began to hear the sound of church bells. Their exultant pealing and clanging grew louder with each step we took. I realized with a flush of pride and joy that all the bells of all the churches of the City of London were ringing out a welcome to us, the victors of Agincourt! All feelings of weariness and disappointment began to ebb from me as I was overcome by a great wave of elation. My pals and I exchanged grins, hardly believing all we were seeing and hearing. People were dancing around us and slapping our backs and offering us gifts! We were heroes! We had done what was expected of us. And, what was more … against overwhelming odds, we had done it brilliantly! Suddenly the death, disease and stench at Harfleur, the freezing rains, the gruelling marching on the broken French roads and the fear and pain on the muddy cornfield all seemed worthwhile. It was at that moment that I remembered my dead father and hoped that I had done him proud.

Now it was time to cross the mighty River Thames and enter the City itself. But this river wasn't blocked as the Somme had been. London Bridge lay open before us and, as trumpets and drums sounded their welcome, I looked up to see that the bridge's massive towers had been decorated in our honour. A giant statue was mounted on each of them; one a sentry, as tall as the towers themselves, who in his left hand held an axe and in his right the keys to the city. The other was a woman, dressed in scarlet and holding out a wreath of gold and silver laurel leaves. But then we crossed the bridge and my eyes almost popped from my head. Spanning the street ahead was a crimson arch beneath which stood hundreds of little choirboys and girls, all dressed in white robes, their faces painted gold and angels' wings upon their backs. They were singing an anthem to the King so sweetly that tears welled up not only in my own fourteen-year-old eyes, but in those of many weary, battle-hardened old soldiers who marched by my side.

"If I didn't know better, I'd swear I'd died and gone to Heaven," grunted Wynn Vaughn, as his own eyes grew wet and shiny.

We climbed a winding cobbled hill and passed between very many poor and dilapidated houses that all stood close-packed. However, the wretched state of their homes didn't stop the ragged and filthy inhabitants of these slums from lining the streets and cheering us until they were hoarse. As their hurrahs continued to ring in our ears we came to a tower draped with shimmering crimson cloth. At the tower's base the cloth had been pegged out to create a pavilion and inside this were many old men dressed as characters from the Bible. As we passed they released flocks of little birds which had all been dipped in gold paint, making them glitter and flash as they swooped about us and occasionally even landed on our heads.

Finally we came to the cathedral of St Paul's, so huge that I think you could fit the whole of Tregarth into it twice over and still have room for the meadow at the back of my mother's cottage. Here, men came out and bowed to the King and girls in white robes blew tiny golden leaves towards him and danced on the steps. At the same time, small boys in a golden wooden castle threw silver laurel leaves and streamers. The King dismounted and walked into the churchyard. Then, accompanied by his bishops and his attendants, he went up the steps and into the cathedral where he knelt before the altar and gave thanks to God. Then accompanied by his royal party, he emerged into the streets and made his way to his palace at Westminster where a great banquet awaited him.

But no such royal feast awaited us, the common soldiers, and it was here then that our procession finally ended. As the crowds continued to cheer, we began to break up into our smaller groups. After saying fond farewells to the comrades-in-arms we had marched with and fought alongside for so many long months, we began to wander off in search of food and lodgings for the night, before beginning our long trek home the following morning.

We may not have been invited to the royal banquet but we certainly drank and ate like kings that night. It seemed that all London was eager to hear of our experiences and, as a result, we didn't once put our hands into our own purses. As we sat in alehouses and inns, complete strangers came up to us, offering to buy us drink and food if only we would tell them of our adventures. So, while Wynn told the story of the siege at Harfleur, the crossing of the Somme and the charge of the French knights at Agincourt over and over again, the Bowens and myself simply sat by and grinned and nodded as we tucked into the good food and drink we had craved for so many months. And that night we finally had the luxury of sleeping under a roof for the first time in months. Our tavern beds might not have been the sort that the King and his nobles were used to but, after the fields and ditches of France, they might as well have been! Then, the next morning, having collected our pay and bought ourselves new winter clothes and boots, we left London and began our march home to Tregarth.

Epilogue

December 1415

And now, as you will have no doubt guessed, my story is almost over. All that remains to tell you of is our homecoming, which was truly joyful, but also deeply sad. During our homeward march the weather was bitterly cold and we were frequently caught in freezing blizzards. But fortunately news of the victory at Agincourt had spread the length and breadth of the land, so at each village we came to we were once more greeted like heroes and offered good food and drink and warm beds for the night.

On the evening of the twelfth day of our trek we finally reached the lane that leads through the woods to our village and I smelled the scent of log fires and heard the village dogs bark at our approach. The moon was full and the sky almost cloudless but large white flakes still occasionally drifted gently through the bare trees to settle on the frosted layer of snow which my new boots crunched across so satisfyingly. As I heard the owls hoot and saw the woodsmoke from the cottage chimneys of Tregarth rise above the trees my heart leaped with joy at the thought that I would soon be reunited with my loved ones. But then I remembered that two of our number were no longer with us. One, I hoped, would be snug and safe in his parents' cottage but the other, I knew, lay dead and gone in a miserable grave pit by a marsh in a distant foreign land. As I remembered poor Harry I was once more struck with terrible pangs of grief for the pal I'd left behind and would never see again.

As we crossed the wooden bridge by the church, I saw lights flickering in doorways and shadowy figures emerging from cottages. A moment later I was surrounded by the people I care for more than any in the world. As cheeks were kissed, tears of joy shed, and hands shook, we asked the questions that had been uppermost in our minds for so long.

"Did Evan return safely from Harfleur?" Owen asked.

"Yes, thank God, he did," his mother told us. "But he is still too ill to leave his bed."

"And how did Harry's parents take the news of his death?" I asked my sister.

"Very badly," she answered. "But at least they have

his five brothers and sisters to love and they were proud to know that their son had died so bravely."

"Did you get news of us at all?" asked Morgan.

"Hardly a thing," replied our village priest. "And, like many people throughout the land, at one point we truly believed that every single one of you had perished at the hands of the French."

"And how has the harvest been?" asked the ever-practical Wynn.

"Good, but we sorely missed six strong pairs of helping hands," replied his wife with a laugh.

It became too cold to stand talking on our village green like this and we all agreed to go our separate ways. So Wynn, Owen, Morgan and I finally took our leave of each other, promising to meet the following morning and visit our sick friend. We then made our way to our homes where we were soon sitting by blazing log fires, recounting the stories of all the astonishing things that had happened to us during our great adventure. And none of us had need to make up or add anything to any of our stories because the things we had seen and experienced in the past five months were in themselves so remarkable and memorable. All they needed was straightforward telling to keep our friends and families wide-eyed with amazement and wonder for weeks and months to come.

And I've a feeling that, as the centuries pass and the world changes, and when I am long gone from this earth, this story of mine will still be told over and over again and will never be forgotten.

Historical note

Between 1337 and 1453, England and France were involved in the series of conflicts, all fought on French soil, which eventually became known as the Hundred Years' War. This war wasn't continuous but consisted of outbreaks of fighting followed by truces which would then be followed by yet more conflict.

The War had its origins in the invasion and conquest of England by the Norman king, William the Conqueror, back in 1066. After William's triumph over the Saxon King, Harold, at the Battle of Hastings in 1066, England was ruled by a series of monarchs, all of whom were related to the French royal family. Consequently, in addition to ruling England, large areas of France were also ruled by these Norman kings and their successors, the Angevins and the Plantagenets.

During the decades between the Norman conquest of England and the outbreak of the Hundred Years' War, family connections between the French-speaking English kings and their royal French relatives became increasingly hostile. Despite the passage of more than two centuries, several English kings who were descended from William the Conqueror still clung to the idea that they had the right to rule large parts of France, if not the whole country.

The first of these French-English kings was Edward III. In 1337 Edward III he said he had the right to be King of France because he was the nephew of the French King, Charles IV, who had just died. But the French weren't too keen on the idea of being ruled by an English king, so King Charles' other nephew, Philip VI, was made the new King of France.

In 1337 Edward III declared himself the rightful King of France (a title claimed by English kings up until 1801). On 26th August 1346 he met the French at the Battle of Crécy where he beat them soundly, despite being vastly outnumbered. As with Agincourt, it was the skill of Edward's archers that won the day as they brought down hundreds of heavily armed French knights with their hail of arrows. As a result, Edward gained the French port of Calais which increased his control over the Channel.

Ten years later, at the Battle of Poitiers, Edward's son, the Black Prince, beat the French, despite being trapped and outnumbered. Again, this victory owed all to the prowess of the archers. King Edward had been one of the first to recognize the usefulness of the longbow when he had observed how the archers of south Wales used it to great success against his own troops. He decided to make sure that his own archers were proficient in the use of this phenomenal weapon and decreed that all men and boys throughout the land must regularly practise their archery skills, even banning the playing of football to make sure they did so.

In 1377, Richard II became King of England. At this point in the Hundred Years' War the French had retaken many of their territories and pushed the English back as far as Calais. Richard's cousin, Henry Bolingbroke, had him killed and took his throne, becoming King Henry IV. Meanwhile, over in France King Charles VI became subject to phases of madness and various nobles began plotting and counterplotting to overthrow him. King Henry IV's own home situation wasn't much better. He was fighting against rebel armies in Wales and Scotland and, to make matters worse, the Black Death had been raging through Britain, killing almost half the population.

Helping King Henry IV out in his battles against the rebellious Welsh and Scots was his eldest son Henry, Prince of Wales, who had been born in 1387.

Henry was a natural warrior. At the age of fourteen he had fought against the forces of the Welsh chieftain Owen Glyn Dwr and at sixteen he commanded his father's forces against the Welsh at the battle of Shrewsbury where he was wounded by an arrow in the face.

On the death of his father in 1413, Henry became King Henry V. In 1415 he told the French King, Charles VI, that he wished to marry his daughter Catherine, and wanted the territories of Normandy and Anjou into the bargain. Charles VI refused and Henry declared war on France – and so the next phase of hostilities in the Hundred Years' War began.

Henry assembled his army, consisting of troops from England, Wales, Germany, Ireland and Flanders, then crossed the Channel. His idea was to take the port of Harfleur and use it as a base for his operations, his ultimate objective being to conquer the French capital, Paris, and become ruler of all France. Of course, things didn't go entirely according to plan but, despite being hugely outnumbered at Agincourt, the fantastic skill of the King's archers, many of whom were just boys aged between twelve and seventeen, won the day.

Between 1417 and 1419 Henry followed up this

success with the conquest of Normandy. Consequently, in 1420, King Charles VI signed a treaty saying that on his death Henry V would become King of France. The following month Henry married King Charles's daughter. However, many of the French nobles in the southern part of the country didn't want Henry as king so in 1421 he returned to France to continue fighting them. Whilst besieging the town of Meaux in 1422 he fell victim to the disease that had killed so many of his men at Harfleur and died of the bloody flux on 31st August 1422. His flesh was boiled from his bones which were then taken back to England to be buried at Westminster Abbey.

Over the next ten years almost all of the territory Henry had conquered was lost again when Charles VI's son and a French peasant girl called Joan of Arc led the French against the English again driving them back to their stronghold at Calais.

The story of the Battle of Agincourt soon became the stuff of legend, with William Shakespeare basing his famous play, *King Henry V* on the battle. In later years, the Welsh author, Arthur Machen, wrote his "Angels of Mons" story, in which the archers of Agincourt return to save trapped and outnumbered British troops in World War One.

Timeline

Early summer 1415 Men are mustered to form King Henry V's army. They begin to march to Spithead. Meanwhile, the King assembles his huge war-fleet.

10 August Soldiers and supplies are boarded and King Henry V's invasion fleet closes up at Spithead.

11 August The invasion fleet departs Spithead.

14–18 August The fleet anchors near Harfleur and the army disembarks.

30 August Bloody flux has a terrible grip on army.

7 September The French are desperate and fight recklessly to defend Harfleur.

15 September Fiercest bombardment of Harfleur so far.

16 September A truce is called.

22 September The French finally surrender.

5 October King Henry's army leaves Harfleur.

11 October The army reaches Arques and is halted by cannon fire.

13 October A captured French prisoner tells King Henry that all the crossings on the Seine are blocked and 6,000 French troops are shadowing his army.

15 October The men's rations are all used up. They eat wild nuts and berries.

17 October A group of archers are trampled during a French cavalry ambush. The King orders the archers to cut long stakes from the hedgerows.

18 October The King's army spends the night at Nesle where the locals tell him of an unguarded crossing on the River Somme.

19 October The army successfully crosses the Somme.

21 October The army comes upon the tracks of thousands of men and horses near the town of Peronne.

24 October The army reaches the ridge at Blangy and sees the huge host of French knights, artillery and foot soldiers, possibly totalling 60,000.

25 October (St Crispin's Day) The Battle of Agincourt takes place.

26 October King Henry's army leaves Agincourt and begins the march to Calais.

16 November The King's army crosses the English Channel.

23 November They reach London and receive a heroes' welcome.

Picture acknowledgements

P172 Portrait of Henry V National Portrait Gallery, London,
         UK/Bridgeman Art Library
P173 French knight on horseback, Mary Evans Picture Library
P174 Medieval arms and armour, Mary Evans Picture Library
P175 Manuscript illumination, AKG London/British Library

A portrait of King Henry V.

A Medieval French knight and warhorse.

A French painting showing Henry V's army at the Battle of Agincourt.

Different types of armour and weapons used by the English in the fourteenth and fifteenth centuries.

Also in the series:

BATTLE OF BRITAIN
The Story of Harry Woods
England 1939-1940

THE TRENCHES
The Story of Billy Stevens
The Western Front 1914-1918

CIVIL WAR
The Story of Thomas Adamson
England 1643-1650

TRAFALGAR
The Story of James Grant
HMS Norseman 1799-1806

ARMADA
The Story of Thomas Hobbs
England 1587-1588

CRIMEA
The Story of Michael Pope
110th Regiment 1853-1857

ZULU WAR
The Story of Jabulani
Africa 1879-1882

INDIAN MUTINY
The Story of Hanuman Singh
India 1857-1858